When Mary Met the Colonel

A Pride and Prejudice Novella

Victoria Kincaid

Contents

Chapter 1

"La, Colonel! Regimentals do make a man ever so dashing!"

Colonel Fitzwilliam hid his wince. If Miss Kitty Bennet's voice grew any shriller, it would soon be audible only to dogs. He was not certain how to respond to such a comment. Should he thank her or modestly deny it—when he really wished to beg her to leave him in peace?

Grabbing his elbow, she pulled Fitz toward her. He gently extricated his arm from her grasp once more, only to have it captured again within moments. Napoleon's generals could learn tactics from Kitty Bennet. Why did urgent dispatches from his commanding officer never arrive when he needed them? Or attacks of apoplexy?

Fitzwilliam yielded the field to Miss Kitty for the moment and glanced about the Longbourn drawing room, crowded with guests for the wedding breakfast celebrating the marriage of his cousin, Fitzwilliam Darcy, and Kitty's sister, Elizabeth Bennet—now Darcy. Perhaps the joy of the occasion would wash away his irritation. Indeed, it was an excellent match, and the couple appeared very happy.

But his momentary happiness was immediately dampened by the sense of impending dread at the sight of Maria Lucas crossing the room with an air of determination. No doubt he was her target. Another girl mad for a red coat, Miss Lucas had been at odds with Miss Kitty over Fitz since his arrival the day before. They appeared to believe the matter was to be settled by them without any input from Fitz.

Kitty also saw her rival's approach and sought to draw his attention to her. "Did you bring your sword today, Colonel?"

"No. Generally speaking, weddings do not provide occasions to run people through." Miss Kitty laughed as if it were the cleverest thing she had ever heard. This time, Fitz did wince at the shrill sound.

Miss Lucas finally reached them, slightly out of breath. "Colonel, would you care to dance?" She fluttered her eyelashes. He supposed many men would consider her pretty, but he found the vapidity of her expression and the artificiality of her manner completely unappealing.

He frowned at her. "There is no music."

Miss Lucas shrugged. "Mary will play the pianoforte. I shall make her."

What a treat for Mary, Fitzwilliam thought. "I do not believe there is space for dancing at the present, Miss Lucas."

The girl pouted for a moment but then smiled coyly. "Then would you care to take a turn about the garden?"

Miss Kitty used her hold on his elbow to yank him closer. "He promised to take me for a tour of the garden!" She scowled at the girl whom yesterday she had declared her closest friend in the world.

I did? I must not have been present for that part of our conversation.

Fitz made a show of peering through the crowd. "I do believe Darcy is seeking me out. I pray you, pardon me." He firmly disengaged Miss Kitty's hand from his arm and evaded a renewed attempt at capture.

"Where? I did not see him!" she cried petulantly.

Rather than respond, Fitz plunged into the crowd. His only hope lay in speed; if he slowed his pace, the enemy would be upon him immediately. The French should hire the two girls as scouts; they had an uncanny knack for spotting red coats. Fitz slipped between two groups of people in the crowded room, hoping that any pursuers would lose sight of him.

After another minute of frantic maneuvering from room to room, he appeared to have shaken anyone on his trail and permitted himself a relieved exhale. The two girls had occupied all of his time since he had arrived at Longbourn, and he was weary of hearing how well gold buttons set off a red coat and how worthy cavalry officers were.

Ah, the back door to the house—just what Fitz required. Upon exiting, he spied Darcy in the garden speaking with Bingley, who had married Elizabeth Darcy's sister, Jane, a month earlier. As Fitz approached, Bingley nodded a greeting, but his attention was immediately occupied by the simultaneous arrival of his wife at his side.

Fitz took advantage of the opportunity to seize his cousin by the elbow. "Why did you not warn me that I was walking into an ambush?" he asked through gritted teeth.

Darcy laughed and tossed down the remainder of his glass of champagne. "Why would I? Surely your commanding officers would agree that you need practice in evading capture."

Fitz was too provoked to laugh. "If I had guessed at their persistence, I would not have worn my regimentals. I would have been better served with a disguise."

Darcy grinned at him. "Do not act so put out, my friend. I know you love the attention."

Fitz scowled. "I did once, but not now. I am no longer enamored of girls who flirt and simper."

"Oh?" Darcy arched a brow at him.

Fitz did not mind forcing his cousin to bear the brunt of his foul mood. "It grew tiresome long ago."

Darcy nodded, staring at his now-empty glass. "I am sorry." There was nothing more his cousin could say.

Unexpectedly, Darcy's eyes came alive with a blazing light. Without looking, Fitz knew that his cousin was gazing on his wife, Elizabeth. He also knew that her face would be alight with an equal passion.

A familiar nausea churned in Fitz's gut, and he rubbed the back of his neck to ward off an impending headache. Unfortunately, he had become all too familiar with these sensations recently.

Oh, he did not want Elizabeth for himself—although he had once enjoyed flirting with her. No, he wanted the passionate love Darcy shared with her, their easy communication, their very relationship. Fitz would never have thought they were compatible, particularly after the way his cousin had behaved at Rosings. But now he recognized how their strengths and weaknesses complemented each other perfectly.

But Fitz had no hope of finding a similar love. Such a deep, passionate connection happened only once a generation. No, Fitz knew enough of the world to be aware that the best he could hope for would be a nice woman with a modest fortune whom he could rub along with tolerably.

As Darcy gazed soulfully into Elizabeth's eyes, Fitz focused deliberately on a nearby rosebush, which was more thorns than blossoms—not much of a testament to Mrs. Bennet's gardening skills. Watching them was like staring into the sun. It was beautiful but likely to blind you if you focused on it too long.

From the corner of his eye, Fitz saw movement: Darcy took his wife's hand and tucked it into the crook of his arm. Their eyes did not break the connection the whole time. If Fitz had not been there, would they have kissed?

Suddenly, there was not enough air in this corner of the garden. "Something…to drink…" he murmured as he stumbled away from the happy couple. But he took the path deeper into the garden rather than return to the house.

"Fitz?" Darcy's voice was full of concern; however, Fitz did not stop or slow. His sole focus was escape—escape from both overly amorous newlywed couples and predatory girls.

The garden was larger than he had initially believed. Much of it was overgrown and rather wild-looking. The fashion of the day was for more formal, landscaped gardens in the French style, but Longbourn's garden had probably been designed in an earlier era when more naturalistic styles were in vogue. And then, apparently, it had primarily been left to its own devices. Many of the bushes appeared to have never benefited from the attention of a pair of pruning shears.

However, the tangled vines and bizarrely shaped hedges concealed Fitz from other guests— and the wildness suited his dark mood.

Although Fitz did not begrudge his cousin a moment of happiness, such occasions had become fraught of late. His brother had recently married a beautiful young woman, and now Darcy was leg-shackled as well. His friend John Wright's wedding had been only a few months ago. And although he did not know this Bingley fellow well, he seemed to be enjoying his marital bliss. Everywhere, friends and relatives who had once sustained him through balls and flirtations were settling into the marital state.

And they *all* found these intelligent, well-spoken, steady young ladies, while Fitz only ever attracted the silly ones whose heads were full of foolish tales of the glories of battle and fixated on a dashing figure in regimentals. Perhaps he should be grateful for his uniform since he had nothing else to offer a potential wife; the money from soldiering barely supported him. He loved serving his country, and the work he did was important, but girls like Kitty Bennet and Maria Lucas could not see beyond the uniform. They never expressed any interest in *him*.

Fitz slowed his pace to an amble and brushed his hair from his forehead. It was a warm day for spring, and he enjoyed the sunshine as he followed a meandering path, occasionally framed by overhanging branches and vines.

He gave his head a hard shake. *Enough with this melancholy inner soliloquy. I am not a heroine in a popular novel!* He had no need to provide an heir and no responsibilities to anyone else. If he never married, he would still have a good life. Never mind that the thought generated an aching hollowness in his chest. He would survive; soldiers were trained to survive.

Better never to marry than to marry a superficial chit who chattered on all day about lace and curtains and the cost of a joint of meat. He shuddered at the thought.

The pathway opened unexpectedly into a little clearing with a bench in the center. Fitz stumbled to a stop; the bench was inhabited.

His sudden appearance caused the young woman to start violently and drop her handkerchief. Her head jerked up to see who had disturbed her and immediately tilted down again. It was enough to reveal a pretty face, although perhaps not by conventional standards. Her brown hair was dark and glossy, pulled back in a severe style without any curls around her face. Her nose was a little long and her brows a little heavy for today's fashions, but her mouth…was wide and pink with full, round lips. A mouth made for kissing. *What the hell had provoked that thought?*

"I beg your pardon, miss." Fitz bent to retrieve the handkerchief. Taking it from his fingers, she was careful not to touch him while her eyes remained fixed on the stone of the path. "I did not mean to startle you…" She said nothing, crushing the handkerchief in one hand. "…I believed myself to be alone."

Her eyes flicked up to his face and down again, long enough for him to discern that they were a dark, rich brown—but red-rimmed. "'Tis not your fault. I-I fear I startle easily." Her voice was low and melodious. Fitz would love to hear her sing. If only he could inquire about the source of her tears, but he did not even know her name.

Perhaps he could lead to the subject indirectly. "It appears that we are both seeking a refuge from the crowds in the drawing room."

She said nothing for a moment, but finally, she spoke. "Yes. My sister and her friend wished me to play dance music for them, but there is not enough space for dancing."

Fitz gave a short laugh. "I thought so as well!" He cleared his throat. "You must be Miss Mary Bennet."

The young lady dabbed at her eyes with a corner of the handkerchief, which was still fairly clean despite its tumble to the stones. "Yes. The two elder Miss Bennets are the pretty ones, and the two younger Miss Bennets are the lively ones. I am the one in the middle—neither pretty nor lively." Her hand immediately flew to her mouth. "Oh, dear me! That sounded terribly bitter, did it not? I apologize, Colonel."

Ah, he suspected that he had now uncovered the reason for her tears; such sentiments might be particularly acute on the day one of her sisters married. Fitz took the liberty of seating himself next to Miss Bennet. "Do you fear to offend my delicate sensibilities?" He batted his eyelashes absurdly, provoking laughter. "Only apologize if you are speaking an untruth."

Her lips thinned into a flat line. "No. I always speak the truth."

"No, you do not." This caused her eyes to raise to his face in bewilderment. "You are quite pretty, perhaps not in the same way as your sisters." Mary's lips parted slightly, and she appeared, if anything, even more bewildered. Had no one ever said as much to her? "And if by 'lively' you mean that your sisters chase men wearing red coats, then I am quite pleased you are comparatively sedate." This elicited a giggle from the young lady. "Your presence is quite restful, and so far your conversation is vastly more interesting."

She blinked rapidly at him as if not understanding his words. Surely someone else had thought to tell her how pretty she was? Then a deep blush spread itself over her face and the part of her neck revealed by her gown's neckline, much higher than today's styles. Why did a simple compliment provoke such a reaction?

"Thank you. It is very kind of you to say." Her voice was almost a whisper. Mary fixed her gaze on a number of blossoms in her lap.

"I did not say it to be kind. It is what I observe."

Blushing an even darker red, she glanced about the clearing as if hoping to be rescued from this conversation. She was not only unaccustomed to compliments but also exceedingly shy, Fitz decided. She resembled Georgiana a bit, although Miss Bennet must be at least two or three years older.

Apparently deciding that no help would be forthcoming, she returned her gaze to the hands tangled in her lap. She cleared her throat. "Mr. Darcy said you are recently returned from the peninsula."

Fitz blinked, a bit surprised at the abrupt shift in topic. Did she wish to direct the conversation away from the personal? "Yes."

"I have been following the war in the papers," she murmured. Fitz raised his eyebrows. A woman had never broached this topic with him. "Do you believe those accounts to be accurate on the whole?"

Fitz leaned toward her slightly. "Are you certain you wish to speak about this? Many women find the topic to be…distressing."

A crease formed between her eyebrows. "Sir, the events of this war will affect our country for generations to come. It will influence the futures of my nieces and nephews. Faced with such weighty matters, I do not understand why anyone believes I should care about the latest designs in lace!"

Abruptly, she bit her lip and blushed. "I apologize for that outburst. I have had a trying day. I am overwrought." She stood quickly, straightening her skirts. "I will trouble you no—"

Without forethought, Fitz seized her hand in his. "Please do not leave just when you are proving to be an interesting conversational partner." He remained seated, hoping it would encourage her to stay.

"I think I must." She stared at the ground.

"Miss Bennet, if you will allow me to be frank, the majority of my visit has been occupied by your younger sister and her friend admiring the fine handiwork of the buttons on my uniform." Her shoulders shook; had he provoked laughter? "Intelligent conversation about the happenings in the world would be quite welcome."

Slowly, Mary's head lifted. Her eyes traveled down her arm, paused on her hand—which he had not released—and then rose to meet his eyes. Whatever she saw there caused her body to soften slightly. Fitz took the opportunity to tug on her hand, encouraging her to sit once more.

It was wildly inappropriate to be holding her hand, although they both wore gloves. If anyone should happen upon them, their proximity could lead to all sorts of difficulties, including an accusation of compromising her reputation. Yet he could not bring himself to leave; he was too intrigued to allow the conversation to end.

She allowed him to pull her down on the bench beside him, and he instantly released her hand. "I pray you, ask your questions." Mary regarded him warily, a wild animal that might be easily startled. "What did you wish to ask me?" he asked gently.

"Did you fight at Salamanca?" He nodded. Her eyes lit with interest. "The papers all claimed Wellington's strategy was brilliant, but they never described the details. What did he do?"

Fitz was momentarily in the uncharacteristic position of being at a loss for words. *This* was her most pressing question? He expected a query about the Spanish people or Wellington's character. Instead, she asked about…battle strategy?

"Well…he held some of his troops in reserve until later in the battle," Fitz finally responded, an accurate but incomplete answer.

Miss Bennet scoffed. "That is a common enough strategy. There is nothing brilliant in that."

Fitz blinked at her. *How did she—?* "Miss Bennet, what *have* you been reading?"

Instantly, her face was aflame, and she ducked her chin. "Do not say as much to my family, particularly my mother, I pray you!"

He nodded; as a rule he avoided conversations with Mrs. Bennet, who was almost as excited about a red coat as her daughter.

Miss Bennet's eyes darted about the clearing, making sure of their solitude. "I have read both Brown's and Gibbon's histories. My father did not miss them from his library, but Mama would be horrified if she knew." Her eyes were now downcast.

What an extraordinary woman!

"With every turn of this conversation, I am more and more amazed," Fitz said.

Miss Bennet wrapped her arms around her waist. "I know it is not what a proper young lady would read."

Fitz was horrified that she perceived these interests as a character deficiency but struggled to keep his tone light. "Perhaps more young ladies should read such subjects; I would far rather discuss military strategy than lace." He did not garner the laugh he sought, but she rewarded him with a small smile.

Fitz stood. "If you have read Brown and Gibbon, a simple explanation of the strategy at Salamanca will not do. I will need to explain the terrain around the city." He cast his eye about the clearing. "Here." He gestured her to the side of the clearing, a small area of dirt not covered by the stone underfoot. With a stick, he drew a line in the dirt. "So, here is the city." He made an X. "And these are Wellington's troops…" She watched with rapt attention. It was very pleasant to have such an enthusiastic audience. "The French troops were here and here…"

***

"But why did he not attack from the left flank?" Mary asked the colonel, her eyes fixed on the crude map he had drawn in the dirt as she imagined troops and canons and the chaos of battle.

"They did not have time to mount an effective attack. Nor did they have the numbers of troops they needed," the colonel responded, bending to scratch another line in the dirt. "By then the French were in full retreat."

Mary nodded. It was all so interesting! Accounts in the papers tended to be simple recitations of facts. However, the colonel brought to life the personalities, the strategies, the sights, and the sounds of the battle. "Were you at Ciudad Rodrigo?

The colonel straightened up, exhaling a little laugh. "I was, but perhaps we should reserve that discussion for another day. I should return to the drawing room before I am missed."

Glancing up at the sun, Mary realized only now that they must have talked for more than an hour. Nobody would think anything of her absence—they only wanted her to play the pianoforte —but if anyone suspected that she had been alone with the colonel, it could cause difficulties. His kindness and patience should not be rewarded with accusations and scandal.

Her hand flew to her mouth. "Of course! I quite forgot myself. I should not occupy all your time when you—"

He interrupted. "Please believe it was my pleasure. I would enjoy continuing the conversation later."

His eyes caught and held hers, but she quickly focused on her shoes. Throughout their conversation, she had avoided his direct gaze. Although many would not have called him handsome, his face was open and amiable, and his deep green eyes were entirely too mesmerizing. When he moved his head, the sun caught reddish hints in his dark brown hair. It would be all too easy to make a fool of herself.

"Yes, of course," she murmured. Naturally, he must say such things to be polite.

"Miss Bennet." His voice was firm as he placed a finger under her chin and lifted her head so she must meet his eyes. "I am perfectly sincere. There are few people outside the military with the grasp of strategy you have displayed here. It is astounding."

"I merely read a lot," she mumbled, freeing her chin from his grasp and pulling away.

"Hmm…" She could almost feel the heat of his gaze on her. "I understood from your sister that you mostly read religious texts."

She ducked her head. "I hide Brown and Gibbon behind a copy of Fordyce's *Sermons* when I read; Fordyce is quite a large book. I quote a few passages upon occasion so no one will suspect I have not read the entire volume. It really is dreadfully dull stuff."

Fitz laughed, his green eyes sparkling. "You are quite a surprise, Miss Bennet!"

She regarded him sidelong. "It is terribly unladylike…"

"Not at all. Why should young ladies be expected to read a book that would put most clergy to sleep?" Laughter erupted from Mary, and she quickly covered her mouth, but her eyes were dancing. "Your secret is safe with me," the colonel promised.

"Thank you." She wished to ask the colonel much more but deliberately closed her lips to prevent any words from emerging. She had probably spoken more to the colonel than she had to any man, save her father. Mama always warned that men did not like women who talked excessively— which was rather hypocritical of her.

"I must return to the wedding breakfast." The colonel managed a show of great reluctance. He had wonderful manners and was very good at making a woman feel important. Some woman would be lucky to be his wife.

"Yes, of course. I will follow in ten minutes." That would preclude any possible scandal.

He opened his mouth, then closed it, then opened it again. "I hope we may speak again."

"Certainly, if you wish."

"I do." Before she understood what he was about, the colonel took her hand, kissed the back, and disappeared up the path to the house. The pressure of his lips on her hand lingered even as she brought it up to rub her cheek. She sighed. No man had ever bothered to kiss her hand before. It would be a very nice memory to cherish on long, cold nights alone in her bed.

Chapter 2

All the things I could tell her about Ciudad Rodrigo….

"Colonel, are you feeling well?"

"Hmm?" Fitz looked up from his breakfast plate at Bingley. "Perfectly well, thank you." Why was Bingley inquiring?

"That was the third time I asked." Bingley chuckled.

Fitz rubbed his forehead with one hand. "I apologize. I am not the best of guests. Perhaps I am overly tired."

"Yesterday was a long day," Mrs. Bingley said graciously as she poured him more tea. "I am certain Elizabeth and William were quite fatigued by the time they reached London, but they did not wish to delay their departure."

Bingley smiled at his wife over the rim of his tea cup. "I believe most newly married couples prefer to be alone."

Mrs. Bingley blushed but said nothing. Fitz had the sense of being outside in the cold, watching a family enjoying a warm Christmas dinner. *Do not be bitter. You have a rewarding career, food, a roof over your head, and good friends and family. It is more than many have.* Somehow, such admonishments did not improve his spirits.

"I apologize that I could not secure a place in the post carriage for a departure today," Fitz told his hosts. "It is very good of you to have me another day."

"Think nothing of it!" Bingley responded. "We are quite pleased to have you visit. Darcy has mentioned you often, and I am happy to make your acquaintance at last."

"And I you," Fitz said. Bingley was quite an amiable fellow and seemed well-suited to his wife.

Mrs. Bingley cut into her sausage. "Will you be going abroad again soon, Colonel?"

Fitz nodded. "I expect so."

Bingley's eyes lit with interest, but he said nothing. Fitz guessed that he preferred not to discuss the war in his wife's presence.

She nodded. "My sister Lydia's husband is in a Northern regiment. She expects he will be ordered abroad soon."

Fitz said nothing. The Bingleys obviously did not know that he had helped secure Wickham's commission, and Fitz had no desire to enlighten them. He sought a less fraught subject for the conversation. "How will your parents fare with only two daughters at home?"

Mrs. Bingley smiled gently. "It will be quite an alteration for them. Until recently, we were all five at home, and now three are gone within a short span of time. At least I am close here at Netherfield."

"Have any of your other sisters formed attachments?" He cleared his throat, unsure why his voice cracked when he asked such an innocuous question.

"None that I am yet aware of," she responded. "But Kitty is always out and meeting new people. Mary is more retiring."

Fitz frowned. Why did nobody give Mary the credit she deserved? "I had a very pleasant conversation with Miss Bennet yesterday."

Bingley's eyebrows shot up. "Miss Mary Bennet? Are you sure?"

"Indeed, I have no difficulty differentiating the two ladies," Fitz said dryly. Mrs. Bingley hid a smile behind her napkin.

"Are you much interested in theology?" she inquired.

"No, we discussed—" Abruptly, Fitz remembered that Mary's interest in military history was a secret. "Uh…history…and the events of the day. It seems she reads the papers a great deal."

Mrs. Bingley's eyes widened. "Indeed? I thought she only read Fordyce's Sermons."

How was it that even Miss Bennet's own sister did not know of her true cleverness? The poor woman was even more sadly misunderstood than he had first thought.

He found himself wishing to speak with her again. Soon he would return to London where the women of the ton only discussed gossip and gloves or sought to please his vanity—when they deigned to notice a second son at all. How lovely it would be to have one more conversation with a woman of intelligence before returning to such dreariness! But how could it be contrived? He was scarcely acquainted with the Bennet family; calling upon them would surely bring him unwanted attention from Miss Kitty.

"Do you plan to visit Longbourn today, Mrs. Bingley?" he asked, hoping he sounded casual.

She set down her fork. "I should. Mama's nerves will be in a state after the excitement yesterday."

He vowed to discover some means to manage Kitty. "I would be happy to accompany you and thank your parents for their hospitality yesterday."

"That would be very pleasant," she responded. "Charles, shall you join us?"

"I believe I will."

Fitz could not account for the sudden rapid beating of his heart.

***

Mary was usually not fond of walking, but today, escape from Longbourn had taken on an urgency usually reserved for house fires or attacking highwaymen. Her mother had shrieked about her nerves. Her father had grumbled about her mother's shrieking. Kitty had complained vociferously about the grumbling and shrieking.

Mary had not even consumed breakfast before taking refuge on the path to Oakham Mount. Her walk lasted as long as she could manage, but the day had turned warm, and now she was hungry and thirsty. Reluctantly, she determined that it was time to return home.

During the walk, a depressing realization had swept over her: Longbourn would be worse than ever now. Now that her other sisters were married, Mary had hoped that she and Kitty would grow closer, but Kitty had quickly dispelled that illusion. Before dinner the previous evening, Mary had joined in Kitty's conversation with Maria Lucas.

"No one wishes to hear what you have to say," Kitty had declared. "Go read some sermons or something." Then she and Maria had giggled.

After dinner, Mary had swiftly departed for her solitary room, where she could pretend such words did not wound her.

She arrived at the place where the path to Oakham Mount curved around a small hill and joined the main road to Longbourn. Stepping onto the road, Mary was surprised to notice three figures in the distance, walking from the direction of Netherfield.

"Mary!" one of the figures waved and called.

Oh! It was Jane and Mr. Bingley. *And the colonel!* Abruptly, Mary's heart thudded against her ribs. She was not prepared to see the man again so soon. Could her constitution withstand it?

Did it matter? Barring an unexpected earthquake or pirate attack, she had no choice.

Soon the others reached her, and greetings were exchanged. "We are on our way to Longbourn," Jane informed her.

"Then we shall walk together," Mary said, clasping her hands behind her back.

The four started walking as a group but eventually formed two couples. The colonel showed as little desire to reach Longbourn as Mary had, and the Bingleys were soon far ahead.

Now that she saw the colonel again, Mary was reminded of the unusual intimacy in their previous conversation—despite its subject matter. As a consequence, she felt more than a little awkward in his presence. They made do with a few minutes' conversation about the unseasonably warm weather and the lovely wedding breakfast. Then there was a long pause.

"The past months have been quite eventful for your family. Your parents may be pleased with some quiet," the colonel observed.

Mary kept her eyes fixed on the road. "I suppose. Things will be quite different now that Elizabeth, Jane, and Lydia are gone."

"Your parents must be happy that you and your sister remain."

Mary shrugged. "Lydia is Mama's favorite, and Elizabeth is Papa's, so they will both have to settle for us."

The colonel seemed a bit taken aback at her frankness. *Why do I say such things? He has no desire to hear about my small troubles when he will soon be returning to the field of battle.*

She opened her mouth to apologize, but then he spoke. "Forgive me, but why are you not someone's favorite? You should be!"

He was well-versed in flattery, just as all gallant gentlemen, but the words still warmed her heart. "That is very kind of you to say."

He frowned. "I do not believe in idle flattery."

Mary restrained an impulse to shake her head. Perhaps he believed what he said, but she could not allow herself to credit such words—although part of her soul wished to soak them up as the ground soaks up rain.

"Are you close to your sister, Miss Kitty?" the colonel asked.

"We are only a year apart in age," Mary responded, knowing that was not what he meant.

"Are you good friends?" he persisted.

Mary pressed her lips together. She did not wish to complain, nor did she wish to lie to this dashing young man. *What could I say?* Silence stretched between them.

The colonel gave her a sidelong glance, and Mary suppressed a secret thrill. "Perhaps you and Kitty will be closer now that Lydia is gone."

Mary stopped briefly to pluck a wild flower from the side of the road. "We are quite different in temperament."

His gaze returned to the road before them, but a corner of his mouth quirked up. "Indeed." Silence reigned as they continued their stroll. Finally, the colonel said, "Perhaps you will not be at home long. You are of marriageable age."

Why did her heart leap to hear such a commonplace observation coming from this man?

Her hand crushed the petals of the flower. "I do not have any expectations in that regard."

"Why not?" He looked genuinely perplexed.

She had been overly candid with him; why stop now? Most likely she would never see the man again. "I am plain, quiet, and dull—with no dowry to speak of. I expect I will never marry."

The colonel stopped so suddenly that it startled her, and he seized her arm. "Plain! Plain? And dull? Of all the—do not say such things about yourself! Why, you are one of the prettiest, most interesting women I have had the pleasure of encountering in my life."

Mary's mind was blank for a moment. *Could he possibly believe what he said? Or was it more empty flattery?* He seemed genuinely distressed that she disparaged herself, but nobody had ever said such words to her. She had expected to live her entire life without hearing such things.

No, I cannot afford to believe such compliments; it is too dangerous to nurture any hopes. Mary gave a short laugh and turned her gaze away.

He grabbed her by the shoulders and forced her to gaze into his eyes. "Listen to me, Mary Bennet! You may not be conventionally beautiful, but you are quite pretty enough to attract your share of attention—particularly if you take more care with your appearance. Certainly men who seek an empty-headed chit would not be interested, but you would be wasted on such men!"

He released her abruptly and stalked down the road toward Longbourn, kicking up a cloud of dust from the road. Mary stood frozen, her feet—and whole body—unable to move. *Do I dare believe he is in earnest?* There might be one man—a handsome, intelligent man—who found her attractive and interesting? She wanted to believe, but belief was so dangerous. However, she did know that she must speak with him.

His long strides had already carried him quite a distance; she raced to follow. She was panting by the time she caught up with him. "You-you do not mean that!"

He turned his head sharply. "Do I not?" His tone was almost angry. But then he stopped, lowering his head and taking a deep breath. "I must marry a woman of means. I am a second son." Mary nodded, not sure where his conversation was leading. She had expected as much. "But if I did not—if I were Darcy or Bingley—I would consider paying court to you, Mary Bennet." Mary gasped.

His fingers reached up and gently caressed her cheek. She closed her eyes, savoring the soft touch on her skin. When she opened them again, he had stepped away.

"You should be proud of yourself! Show others the best of yourself!" His voice was fierce and commanding, reminding her forcefully that he was indeed an army officer. His gaze was uncompromising. "Promise me!"

Mary blinked rapidly, feeling as if she dare not disagree. "I-I promise I will try."

His body lost some of its tension, and his shoulders slumped. "Good. That is all I can ask."

***

The only true complaint Fitz had about his day in Hertfordshire was that it came to an end. At the insistence of Mrs. Bennet, who was probably under the illusion that he was free to marry Kitty, Fitz had remained for dinner. He had fended off some rather intrusive questions from Kitty and ignored quite a few flirtatious glances. Fortunately, Mary had been seated on his other side, so they had enjoyed a lively conversation.

Once when Mary had laughed, Mr. Bennet's eyes darted to them, a most peculiar expression on his face. Was Mary's laughter so rare? Her life at Longbourn did seem rather lonely and dull.

Perhaps when he returned from the peninsula, he would contrive to visit the Bingleys again. Or he might accompany Darcy to visit the Bennets. For the sole purpose of ascertaining how Mary fared. Surely the right man would see through her façade of solemnity and make her an offer.

He ruthlessly suppressed the pang of regret he felt at this thought. Nothing between them was ever possible.

He could not propose to a woman with such meager prospects; they would have almost nothing to live on. Of course, he reminded himself, Mary had not shown any hint of interest in him either. A mutual interest in wars and military strategy was hardly the basis for a love match. What use would she have for an old, broken-down soldier?

Fitz should be happy that she might find a nice country squire while he was away.

And yet somehow he could not quite manage it.

At the end of the evening, the members of the family walked their visitors outside. While the rest of the family stood outside the door and chatted with the Bingleys, Mary turned to Fitz.

"Will you return to battle soon?" she asked.

"I expect to receive orders within a fortnight."

"Back to the peninsula?"

"Yes."

Her face very still, she sucked in a breath. "I pray you will be careful."

"I always am. Luck has been with me so far." Her concern touched a place inside him that he had not known existed.

She swallowed. "I hope…I may…perhaps we shall see each other again when you return."

He was surprised at the strength of his desire as well. "Perhaps at Pemberley."

She gave him a big grin. "Yes, Pemberley!"

He took her hand. "Do not forget what I ask of you." Her brown eyes seemed even darker and more soulful under his scrutiny. "You are worth more."

"I will not forget." Her voice was barely a whisper.

However, Bingley's voice was so loud that it startled Fitz. "Well, Colonel, are you ready to be on our way? Jane would prefer to return while there is still some daylight."

"Yes, of course." Fitz nodded. He squeezed Mary's hand gently before releasing it. "Farewell, Miss Bennet."

"Farewell, Colonel."

Chapter 3

"Pull up to the right! Close ranks! Close ranks, damn it! Get men over there!" Fitz shouted, but he doubted that anybody heard him over the roar of the guns and shouts of soldiers in battle. There was nothing for it; he must ride to the line of skirmish and make them close ranks in person. The major would not be pleased that Fitz had left his post.

The battlefield was a muddy mess, and Caesar, his horse, took his time crossing to the small hill that Fitz's men were attempting to hold. "Close that gap!" he shouted. One man looked up and nodded, but nobody else paid heed. Fitz shook his head and slapped the reins, trying to get Caesar to move faster. If they did not close ranks, Napoleon's troops would soon surge through the gap.

Just as he reached the line, it happened. A small group of French cavalry, shaped like a spearhead, pushed through the line, striking down Burton, the closest of Fitz's soldiers. Fitz could not spare a thought for Burton; he focused on rallying his men to meet the invaders.

He leveled his gun as he shouted orders. "Merritt! Blunt!" Reacting quickly, his men closed in to meet the French, but they were outnumbered. Blunt shot one enemy soldier, who fell from his horse. Gates pulled out his sword to grapple with another. But Merritt took a shot to the arm.

Despite the cacophony of the battlefield, Fitz noticed a particularly loud rifle shot—at close range? A second later, he felt as if a giant had punched him in the chest. Only years in the saddle allowed him to keep his seat on Caesar's back. Looking down, he saw a hole in his uniform, blood welling from it like a fountain and darkening the crimson of the cloth. A minute later, the pain seared through him, and he let out a stream of invective.

He yanked on Caesar's reins to pull back from the front line. A wounded soldier on a horse could be a liability to his comrades. Rather than respond, Caesar jerked and jumped. *Now* the horse chose to be skittish in battle?

Fitz pulled harder, but Caesar did not react, instead lurching to the side. "What the hell?" Fitz muttered. Then Caesar's rear leg collapsed completely. The horse had been shot. Fitz was thrown from the saddle into the battlefield mud. He had no time to move before the rest of Caesar's bulk fell on top of him.

A stabbing pain in his left leg told him that it was broken for sure. But that was not the most immediate danger; he was bleeding and pinned under a dead horse where nobody would discover him. He struggled and pushed, but Caesar was too heavy; he could move neither himself nor the horse. He freed his left hand but was unable to extricate any other part of his body.

Now breathing was becoming difficult. Black spots danced in his vision. *I must escape before I lose consciousness. No one will find me here!*

But his arms and legs were not responding properly anymore. He ordered his hand to push against the horse's corpse, but it barely moved. His vision was quickly tunneling down into nothing.

So this is how it ends, Fitz thought.

He had moments to regret everything he had left undone. He envisioned a pair of soulful brown eyes. Would she ever learn what happened to him? Would she miss him?

His chest hurt abominably, and his leg sent out rhythmic pulses of pain. Fitz tried to focus on something else, anything else. How would he describe the rich color of those eyes? Were they chocolate? Chestnut? Mahogany?

He was still debating as the darkness pulled him down.

***

"Goodbye! Goodbye! We shall see you at the assembly!" Kitty called to the backs of the departing men.

Mary immediately retreated through the front door, knowing Kitty would linger until the young men were out of sight. Benfield and Terry were both nice enough. They were only in the navy, but Kitty had proclaimed it to be almost as good as the army despite the lack of red coats.

In the months since Colonel Fitzwilliam's departure, Mary had changed her hair to a softer, more fashionable style and chosen gowns that were more flattering to her figure. She had done her best to be lively and charming. And she must have succeeded at least a little bit; Thomas Benfield had given her some appreciative smiles and directed at least half of his comments to her. The same thing had happened when John Moore visited last week. Kitty had actually stomped her foot and complained that Mary wanted all the attention for herself.

Mary had almost laughed at the accusation. It was truly a first for her. As if she could take anything from her prettier, livelier sister.

For her part, Kitty was not lacking for company. They had received a number of visits from Louis DeVere, the son of a local viscount, who had made her mother shriek with joy over Kitty's prospects.

When men responded to her attempts at wit and charm, Mary still found herself a bit stunned. Her Uncle Phillips's law clerk had even asked permission to court her, but she found him dull and unattractive and so had asked her father to decline.

Mary also enjoyed company more than she had expected. Banter and flirtation could be pleasing even when the participants were not serious. She danced more and was surprised to find that she enjoyed it. More practice had improved her playing as well; the compliments she received at the pianoforte were the ones she treasured the most. Mary's increased sociability brought her closer to her sister—at least when Kitty was in a good mood. Still, it all took excessive amounts of energy, and she did not understand why Kitty would pursue such activities day after day.

By all rights, she should be thrilled with this newfound attention. And part of her was. But she had discovered that much of it came from men who simply were not to her taste. They could flirt and bestow empty compliments, but none provided the kind of clever, well-informed conversation she sought. Many of the men were quite handsome, but none had that reddish-brown hair or deep green eyes that she could picture in her mind every night before drifting off to sleep.

Honestly, the colonel should never have demanded that she make the effort to meet more men when no other man could ever measure up to him! *He is on the peninsula and made it abundantly clear that he could not court me*, she reminded herself. Although the colonel had declared his attraction to her, part of Mary still wondered if he had merely uttered such words out of pity, knowing he would never be called to act upon them. Even with such doubts, however, she could not stop memories of the colonel from intruding frequently upon her thoughts.

If only she could tell her Mama that she was retiring for the day…but she could not. Her Aunt Phillips was visiting, and Mary must keep her company for at least a little while.

She paused before setting her hand to the drawing room doorknob, listening to ascertain her mother's mood. "And I tell you, Sister, this war is playing havoc with my nerves!" Her mother's shrill voice easily penetrated through the door. "Do you see how my hand is trembling? I worry constantly!"

Mary repressed the urge to snort. Her mother never read news of the war, and no close family members were in battle. Even Mr. Wickham was still in Newcastle. Mary reached out to take the doorknob in her hand.

"Why only today, we received a letter from Lizzy about her husband's cousin—"

Mary's breath caught; she froze with her hand on the knob.

"—Colonel Fitzwilliam. He was grievously injured, and the doctor does not know if he will survive!"

Fortunately, Aunt Phillips spoke immediately, drowning out the sound of Mary's gasp.

Mary only heard her mother's reply. "He was shot, and then his horse fell on top of him, breaking I do not know how many bones! The other men in his regiment found him only just in time. Oh, this war is a terrible business. Cutting down the cream of our young men!"

Mary covered her mouth with her hand to stifle her horrified exclamations.

"Are they bringing him home?" Aunt Phillips asked.

"He should be on a ship now—if he has not already died. He will recuperate at his parents' home in Matlock. Of course, once a man has an injury such as that, he is never the same. Certainly, he will be a shell of his former self."

"Naturally," Mary's aunt said with great authority. "That is always the way of things. Now, tell me where you found that beautiful sprigged muslin."

Mary stumbled back away from the door, all thoughts of entering the room abandoned. Let her mother complain. Something tickled her upper cheek; Mary brushed it away, astonished to find her fingertips wet.

But in the next minute, more tears trickled from her eyes. The thought of the colonel forever maimed from a battle on foreign soil—or, God forbid, already dead— constricted her chest until it was difficult to breath. When she closed her eyes, Mary could see his laughing face, his broad smile, and the tousled hair that never seemed to stay in place. How could someone with that much life and vivacity be forever silenced? It was not possible.

Or, it *should* not be possible.

She had resigned herself that she might never see the colonel again. But at least he would be somewhere in the world living his life. A world that no longer contained Colonel Fitzwilliam? It was too horrible to contemplate. How could life continue without him in it?

It was wrong. So wrong!

Mary knew not how she found her way to her bedchamber, but when she regained awareness of her surroundings, she was huddled on her bed—arms around her knees—a ball of misery.

If only I could do something! Trapped here at Longbourn, she could do nothing to help the colonel. She had no sure way to even receive news about him since no one knew she felt any special attachment. He might now be in Derbyshire, or he might have perished—perhaps on the voyage home. The sense of impotence alone might drive her mad.

At least Elizabeth would have the good fortune to be near him since Pemberley was so close to Matlock. Mary mused on this thought for a moment. Finally, she saw a glimmer of something—perhaps not hope, for she was not ready for hope yet, but at least the beginning of a plan.

She released her legs, dangling her feet over the edge of the bed as she considered this new idea. Yes, she could write to Elizabeth and request an invitation to Pemberley. If the colonel had perished, Mary could do nothing but mourn him. But if he lived, the Darcys would undoubtedly visit him, and perhaps she could accompany them. She knew not how she could be of assistance, but at least she would be there to see him and know he was alive.

It was little enough, but at least it might someday lead to hope.

Chapter 4

Fitz opened his eyes, decided he was hallucinating, and closed them again.

As he assessed himself, however, he actually felt awake and alert. Not at all mired in the febrile dreams he had experienced during his last week in Spain.

Maybe he was not hallucinating.

Cautiously, he opened one eye. No, she was still there. He opened the other eye. The hallucination resembled Mary Bennet—sitting in a chair by the window of his bedchamber, a blue book in her lap. Lit from behind by the waning afternoon sunshine, she almost glowed. Her dress was a plain, pale blue, and the collar was cut lower than he recalled from before—but it suited her beautifully. Her brown hair was gathered in a looser style with delicate curls framing her face.

This was the precise hallucination he would wish to have. Earlier in his life, he might have fantasized about a voluptuous beauty with blonde hair, but at this moment, he could not think of any vision he would prefer.

This was precisely why he remained suspicious. Maybe she was simply a maid who bore a passing resemblance to Mary. But then the woman lifted her eyes from the book and started when she saw him regarding her. For a maid, she stared at him rather boldly.

And smiled a gentle, heart-wrenching smile.

Good Lord, it really was Mary Bennet!

But what was Mary Bennet doing in his bedchamber?

"Why are you here?" *Oh, well said! I might as well have demanded that she leave. Perhaps I should consider a career as a diplomat.*

She furrowed her brow but thankfully made no move to depart. "I shall not tell anyone I was here if you do not."

"But your reputation—" he objected.

She gestured to his leg, which was immobilized by a rope and pulley system suspended from the bed's canopy. The doctor had called the immobilization "traction." Fitz called it a damned nuisance. "I do not believe you are in any position to compromise me." Then she actually giggled. Perhaps she was not the real Mary Bennet despite appearances.

"But just being here…" Fitz pulled the covers up further on his body. Naturally, he was wearing a nightshirt, and the coverlet was almost up to his neck, but still he felt the impropriety most strongly, particularly since his leg could not be covered. During his convalescence, his mother had visited him, of course, and the maids had cared for him, but an unmarried woman of his own class was quite a different matter.

Mary looked down at the floor, a delicate blush covering her cheeks. "I know I should not have slipped in here, but I had to see you myself." She started to stammer. "Y-your mother gave few details about your c-condition." She swallowed. "We only arrived a few hours ago."

"We?"

"Elizabeth and William brought me from Pemberley. I am staying with them for a month." Mary paid particular attention to the lace on her dress.

His mother had said something about the Darcys visiting, but he had only noted it in passing. Between the pain and the frustration of the forced inactivity, his spirits had sunk rather low. The prospect of their visit did little to excite him. However, if his mother had mentioned Miss Bennet, he would have had a different reaction. Fitz ran a free hand through his unruly hair, wincing as the movement pulled on the stitches in his shoulder, and tried to straighten the collar of his nightshirt. What a sight he must present to her!

Mary stood abruptly, glancing at everything in the room but him. "Perhaps I should go. Now that I have seen you…" She briefly met his eyes, her lips slightly parted. "I am happy that you are recovering so well from your injuries."

"No!" The words spilled from his lips before he had a chance to think, but a moment of consideration did not alter his opinion. "I am very pleased to see you. Indeed, very pleased." Mary flushed. "However, if anyone enters, you must be prepared to hide in the closet."

She flashed him a mischievous grin. "I have already deduced that these curtains are sufficient to conceal me." She gestured to the long damask monstrosities his mother had installed recently.

"Yes, that would suit admirably."

She finally resumed her seat, regarding him with a painfully earnest expression. "How are you feeling, Colonel?"

"Much improved now that you are here." He smiled at her.

Other women would have blushed and simpered. Mary scowled. *Why do I find that appealing?* "I am not seeking compliments. I am concerned for your well-being."

Fitz blinked. Truly she was unlike any other woman of his acquaintance. "I spoke the truth. My recovery has been exceedingly dreary. Your presence enlivens my life."

She regarded him suspiciously for a moment; finally, she nodded briskly. "I am happy to be of some use."

Fitz shifted to find a more comfortable position. "Does your leg cause you pain?" she asked. How blunt she was. Most women would direct the conversation away from unpleasant subjects.

He pressed his lips together, planning to deny any pain, but then he noticed her raise her chin a fraction. She was determined to obtain the truth from him. "Sometimes," he allowed.

"It was your shinbone that was broken?" He nodded. "Have you tried walking?"

He shook his head. "I have been on my back since the battle eight weeks ago."

Mary gave him a stern look. "You should practice walking. Even if it is only a few steps."

"But the doctor ordered me not to use it." Fitz struggled into more of a sitting position.

"Doctors who have conducted research on the issue believe it important to start using the leg; it diminishes the likelihood that you will become permanently lame. You should not put weight on it, but moving the knee joint and the rest of the leg will help preserve mobility."

Fitz gaped at her. "How do you know that?"

She stood and opened the blue book to a particular page, then brought it closer to his bedside. "See here?" She pointed to an illustration of a man with his leg elevated in a similar way to Fitz's; another page showed the man walking with the aid of a crutch. "Dr. March found that eight out of ten of his patients recovered more rapidly when they used the broken limb after a period of healing."

Fitz took the book, inspecting the cover and then gazing up at Mary's face. She might have been blushing, but her lips were set in a determined line. "Are you saying you borrowed medical books, as well as military history, from your father's library?"

She did not answer immediately but returned to her seat, where her hand resumed fiddling with the lace trim of her dress. "I bought it in London," she murmured finally. "My father and I stopped to visit family before turning toward Pemberley."

"Are you perhaps considering taking up battlefield medicine?"

She did not respond to his attempt at humor. Her eyes remained fixed on that piece of lace. "I… purchased the books directly before leaving for Pemberley. I asked my father to take me to a store that specialized in scientific and medical books." Her voice was so low that he could barely discern it. "I wanted to know how to help you."

She had purchased and read the book for his sake? Fitz was momentarily unable to speak past the sudden lump in his throat. He swallowed hard. "You purchased more than one book?"

Mary bit her lip, still staring down at her lap. "I also purchased one on bullet wounds and one on treating infections since that appeared to be the biggest danger. Fortunately, your physician seems to be well versed in the latest science on infection." He handed her the book, and she returned it to her lap.

"Yes, the battlefield surgeon was also excellent." Fitz stared in amazement at the small, slight woman by the window. Many—even within her family—would discount or overlook her, not realizing how quietly remarkable she was. His mother had done nothing but wring her hands and fuss since he had arrived at Matlock five days ago. Frustrated with her inability to hasten the healing process, she was driving the doctor and the staff to distraction. Fitz had even occasionally stooped to feigning sleep when she visited the room. His father had done little more than visit and commend his progress on convalescing. It would occur to neither of them to buy a medical book.

Yet here was this young, seemingly unassuming woman who appeared quite gratifyingly worried about him and had educated herself to best help him recover. Fitz's heart swelled with unfamiliar emotions. No one, not even his doctor, had devoted so much thought and effort to Fitz's recovery.

He often contemplated why he had imagined Mary Bennet's eyes as he was on the verge of losing consciousness—on the verge, truth be told, of dying. But it was blazingly obvious. His head was only now catching up to what his heart had realized months ago. He loved Mary Bennet. He was *in love with* Mary Bennet. How had he been blind to it before?

When he had told her that he must marry an heiress, he believed he was warning her against becoming too attached, but *he* was the one who needed to guard against attachment.

And she was here. She had made quite an effort to be at his bedside and help him recover, suggesting that she was not indifferent to him either. Joy coursed through Fitz's veins, and he could not stop his gaze from dropping to her perfect, full lips. How would it feel to kiss her?

In the next moment, however, panic squeezed his heart. *What am I thinking? Nothing has changed.* In fact, his situation had worsened. In all likelihood, he would walk with a limp—if he walked at all—and might never regain the full range of motion in his right arm. Either injury would be sufficient to end his military career, but together...?

He could not contemplate marriage when his future was so uncertain. He had no current means of employment and no prospects. Oh, certainly his parents would continue to provide for him here at Matlock, but these were hardly circumstances conducive to a proposal. His parents had been most opposed to Darcy's marriage to Elizabeth, but at least Darcy had the capacity to support any wife he might choose. Fitz did not have that luxury.

Fitz rubbed his hand over his eyes. Damnation! Why must he realize that he loved her now when she was further out of his reach than ever?

He had never been resentful of his fate as a second son, and his military career had suited him. But his position in life could not provide him with the one thing he wanted so desperately: the woman he loved.

Mary regarded him quizzically. How long had he fallen silent? How many of his feelings had been revealed on his face? He schooled his features into a more amiable mask and regarded her with polite attention.

She met his gaze while simultaneously appearing to shrink back in her chair. "Fortunately, the book on broken limbs is the most recent one. The author is quite certain that complete immobilization of the limb leads to atrophy of the muscle—and thus is the reason some people never walk again."

Fitz raised an eyebrow. "So he would have me walk?"

Mary nodded. "Five minutes of exercise on the first day." She bit her lip. "I know it will be painful, but…"

Fitz shook his head while he struggled to extricate himself from his covers. "No. I am enthusiastic about the idea, Miss Bennet. Forced inactivity is very difficult for a soldier. I would have tried to walk before now if my doctor had not forbidden it."

Mary gave a tentative smile, but her hands still worried the bit of lace on her dress.

"Can you reach the pulley and lower my leg?" he asked her.

Immediately jumping to her feet, Mary reached for the cleat on the wall to which the pulley was tied. Gently she lowered his leg to the bed. Fitz experienced a dull ache but not the searing pain of the first two weeks following his injury.

Using his arms, Fitz pushed himself into a seated position and then swung his legs over the edge of the bed, careful to keep the coverlet over his lap. Mary flushed and studiously looked away. "Perhaps I should call a footman?"

"No. Then my mother would soon be lecturing me about following the doctor's orders. This shall remain between you and me."

Mary bit her lip, but she nodded.

He gestured to her. "I pray you, come closer." She hesitated. "I must lean on you to help me out of bed."

"Oh! Of course!" she cried, hastening to his bedside.

Fitz adjusted his position, setting his feet solidly on the floor. He placed his hand on Mary's shoulder, trying not to notice the warm skin where the dress left her neck bare. Under his hand, she shifted slightly, preparing to bear his extra weight. He leaned forward, putting weight on his right leg, and then straightened his body as much as he could, pushing up on Mary's shoulder. His right leg protested mildly since he had not stood in so long, but his left leg screamed bloody murder. He clamped his lips together against inadvertent cries of pain. It felt like fire was running down his leg, burning his bones to cinders.

He shifted more of his weight to his right leg so his left foot only rested lightly on the floor. The pain abated some, but he did not relish the prospect of moving.

Now that he balanced on his own, Mary stepped away and fetched the crutches that had been leaning in the corner of the room. Fitz attempted to smooth any signs of discomfort from his features, but apparently, he was less than successful.

"Oh!" Mary said as she handed him the crutches. "Are you in very much pain?"

"It is bearable."

The disbelieving look on her face suggested that she was not convinced. "Perhaps you should sit again?"

Fitz raised his chin stubbornly. "Not until I have had a chance to walk."

He tucked a crutch under each arm and leaned forward, resting his weight on them. Instantly, the pain in his leg lessened. He reached out his good leg, which hurt a little, and then moved the crutches forward, bringing the injured leg after. Mary stood next to him, her arm outstretched to keep him from falling. In this fashion, he took four more "steps" across the room, finally coming to rest against an ornately brocaded chair.

Blood pounded in his ears, sweat beaded his brow, and his breath came in gasps. *Good Lord, what a weakling I have become!*

Only after he had stood still for a minute did Fitz feel capable of speaking. "That was more difficult than I anticipated." Even to his own ears, his voice sounded hoarse and wheezy.

"Do you wish to sit for a minute?" Mary gestured to the chair.

Fitz gave a wry smile. "If I sit, I might not stand again without assistance."

"Perhaps you should return to the bed."

He wanted to protest. He had only taken five steps! But he must take five steps for the return to his bed, and he could barely stand. Mary could guess his thoughts. "You do not want to hurry your recovery and cause yourself more harm."

Fitz blew out a breath. "Very well." Awkwardly, he maneuvered himself into a position where he could turn in a circle, using the crutches to balance.

The trip back to the bed was even slower. Following every step, it was necessary to pause and regain his breath. He would have sworn someone had moved the bed further away, but finally, he was able to sink into the mattress's soft embrace. After his heart rate had returned to normal and Mary had elevated his leg once more, Fitz recognized how disgracefully he had performed in front of a young lady whom he wished to impress. His face grew warm.

Mary remained ignorant of his chagrin as she tucked the coverlet around his body. "You did very well for the first time! A very promising beginning."

"I am happy you were pleased," he grumbled.

"And you should be as well," she responded with some asperity. "It was a magnificent effort!" He did not respond, and her smile dissolved. "Are you experiencing discomfort?"

In truth, he barely noticed the shooting pains traveling down his leg. "No, no!" he reassured her. "There was some discomfort as I walked, but I feel fine now." It was only a small falsehood.

"Perhaps you should take some laudanum," she suggested.

Fitz glanced at the clock on the mantel. "The maid will soon be here with my next dose."

"Oh!" Mary's hand flew to her mouth. "I should go."

Fitz did not wish for her to leave, but he also did not want her to be caught in his room. Although the prospect of being forced to marry her was not completely unappealing, he had no desire to tarnish her reputation.

She had collected her book and was striding toward the door by the time Fitz recovered his powers of speech. "Will you come again tomorrow?" he asked.

Mary stopped and turned a shocked face toward him. "But—"

"I will need your help if I am to walk again," he cajoled. "Everyone else does only what the doctor orders." Mary still appeared unconvinced. "I am always alone at this time—every day."

Mary opened her mouth, shut it, and then opened it again. "Very well. I will try to come again tomorrow."

"Thank you." His gaze held her eyes for a moment. Chocolate, definitely.

She turned away quickly, opened the door, and was gone.

Chapter 5

Mary settled into a chair in Colonel Fitzwilliam's sitting room. They had been visiting Woodley Park for five days and—as far as anyone else knew—she had not seen the colonel during that time. In truth, she had slipped into his room every day and helped him practice walking with the crutches. On the second day, she had nearly been caught by a maid bringing him his tea early, and Mary had been prepared to discontinue her visits. But the colonel had looked so crestfallen and pleaded so eloquently that she had agreed to return.

Of course, Mary's brother, Fitzwilliam Darcy, had visited his cousin every day, and Elizabeth had been to see him once despite the awkwardness of visiting his bedchamber. They had been surprised when, that morning at breakfast, the butler had announced that the colonel would like them to visit him in the sitting room adjoining his bedchamber. It was still a small breach of propriety for Mary to be in such close proximity to his bedchamber, but no one commented on it. In fact, the Countess of Matlock had exclaimed how her son's spirits had improved since the Darcys had arrived. Mary hoped her presence had contributed in some small way to that improvement.

Now she was seated opposite the door to the bedchamber while Elizabeth and William shared a settee to her right. Mary fidgeted with her skirt, smoothing the fabric so it would not bunch up and wrinkle. Elizabeth shot her a sidelong glance. Did she suspect Mary's interest in the colonel went beyond a passing acquaintance?

Mary tried to school her features into an expression of indifference.

A footman opened the bedchamber door, and the colonel came through, still hobbling on his crutches but moving more smoothly than he had even the previous day. He maneuvered so confidently, and his color was robust—so superior to the pale, perspiring face on that first day.

Just through the doorway, he paused and gave a slight bow in Elizabeth and Mary's direction. "Ladies, Darcy, so kind of you to join me." He dissembled believably; not so much as a glance betrayed that they had seen each other the day before. Mary quickly bowed her head in case she was blushing once again.

Taking two more steps into the room, the colonel reached a chair and sank into it. The footman brought a small stool on which he could rest his injured leg.

"How wonderful to see you walking again, Colonel," Elizabeth said with a gentle smile.

"I am very happy to be up and about, I assure you!" His wide grin was infectious, and Mary found herself smiling as well. "Someone warned me that my leg would atrophy if immobilized and suggested I walk despite the pain. And the exercise has proven quite beneficial."

The colonel's eyes sought Mary's and quickly darted away. From the corner of Mary's eye, she saw Elizabeth notice the look.

"Someone who was not your doctor then?" William frowned.

"No. He would have me abed still, but I am quite convinced that would have been the wrong approach." The colonel studiously regarded his hands.

"Well, I am quite certain your parents did not advise you so," Darcy said. "Who else have you seen since you arrived here?"

The colonel waved airily. "I do not recall who said it. Perhaps one of the footmen."

"Your footmen are well versed in medical matters, eh?" One of William's eyebrows rose.

"Probably some bit of country wisdom." The colonel leaned back in his chair, attempting to look nonchalant. "People around here are full of old wives' tales. Fortunately, this one happened to be true."

Elizabeth regarded Mary even more speculatively; she knew of the medical texts. Mary quickly asked the first question that occurred to her. "Are you experiencing much pain, Colonel?"

His gaze swept up and caught hers. Those dark green depths both calmed and cheered her. "I did when I first started walking, but now it is mostly a dull ache," he said.

What did the colonel speak of again? All other thoughts seemed to have fled.

Darcy coughed, and the spell was broken. Mary quickly cast her eyes down to the floor. How long had she stared at the colonel? Heavens, she was no better than Kitty, mooning over a handsome man! If she was not careful, others would guess her secret. Even now she could feel William's assessing gaze upon her; no doubt he was noticing her uncharacteristic behavior. She cast about for another subject to fill the conspicuous silence, but her thoughts would only return, again and again, to those dark green eyes.

Relief arrived in the form of a maid entering with a tea service. As Elizabeth poured, the colonel asked his cousin about that year's crops. The conversation soon focused on the weather, and Mary gave an inward sigh of relief.

***

"How convenient that the colonel received the latest medical advice about recovery from a broken limb." Elizabeth's tone was dry.

It was late afternoon; Elizabeth and Mary were alone in the downstairs drawing room for the first time all day. Elizabeth had spoken immediately after her husband had quitted the room.

Mary forced herself to keep her eyes focused on her embroidery. She had recovered her composure since the near-disaster of the morning. "Indeed. It seems to have done him a world of good." She kept her voice low and neutral.

"It is almost as if whoever gave him advice had access to a recent medical text on the subject." The edge in Elizabeth's voice was sharp enough to cut paper.

Mary schooled her features not to react, but inwardly she was cursing herself. If only she had warned the colonel not to speak about it! Elizabeth was too clever.

"The colonel thought it might be an old wives' tale." Mary stabbed her needle into the fabric once more.

Elizabeth sighed loudly and shifted in her seat. "So that was your destination when you pleaded headaches in the afternoon? The bedchamber of an unmarried man?"

Mary stiffened and met her sister's challenging gaze. "Colonel Fitzwilliam is convalescing—hardly in any condition to compromise a woman."

"Being in his room is enough to compromise your reputation." Elizabeth clutched the arms of her chair. "The Bennet family hardly needs another scandal!"

Mary gasped. How could Elizabeth compare her to Lydia?

But then she squared her shoulders; she would not feel ashamed of her actions. "I will not allow a man to suffer needless pain—and possibly even go lame—because of some imaginary threat to my reputation!" Mary threw down her embroidery. "Nobody cares about my reputation anyway."

"William could have explained it to h—"

"I needed to see for myself how bad it was. I needed to see him." Mary's voice went hoarse with emotion. "I had read the books. William had not."

Elizabeth made an impatient gesture. "Very well, that explains your first visit, but you did not confine your visits to a single time, did you?"

Mary's silence was as good as an answer. Elizabeth made an impatient noise and threw her hands in the air.

"He *asked* me to return!" Mary exclaimed, standing suddenly and pacing the room. "He was happy I was there!" *Nobody else is ever happy to see me.*

"He did? He was?" Elizabeth's surprise was almost comical and most definitely unflattering.

"Yes! Some people find my company enjoyable."

Elizabeth held up her hands in a placating gesture. "I did not mean…of course, he enjoys your company, but—"

Mary strode to the window, wishing she could escape through it to the garden outside. The gentle movement of the trees in the wind was soothing, and Mary rested her forehead against the glass. She started when her sister's hand touched her shoulder.

"Richard must marry an heiress," Elizabeth said gently. "He told me so himself."

"I-I have—I do not—I have no expectations of the colonel," Mary stammered.

Elizabeth turned Mary around so she could gaze into her eyes. "I do not wish you to have your heart broken."

"No, no, he would never. I do not think—" Even as she uttered words of denial, Mary realized that a small part of her *had* been hoping that affection for her would grow in the colonel's heart. But it was hopeless. Even if he did develop such feelings, he could never act on them.

"Perhaps it would be best for your peace of mind if you stopped visiting his room, hmm?" Elizabeth's forehead creased with worry as she regarded her sister.

Mary could not meet Elizabeth's eyes, but she nodded. "He is vastly improved and can easily survive without my visits." She knew it was the right decision.

Why did it create such an ache in her chest?

Chapter 6

Fitz sighed and leaned his weight on the windowsill, half-sitting so he could peer out of the window, which overlooked the front of the house. It had been five days since Mary Bennet had ceased visiting him. He did not know why, but Elizabeth had regarded her younger sister suspiciously when they had all conversed in the sitting room. What was he about, having them meet there? Of course, they betrayed themselves. If he had not been so overly eager—so starved for company from others—Mary might still be visiting him daily.

No doubt Elizabeth had chastised Mary about flouting propriety. And Fitz could hardly be angry with her for an unwillingness to risk her reputation. Confined to his room, he could not even see or converse with her unless he asked for another tea in the sitting room.

Now Fitz was limited to hoping for a glimpse of her through the window as she exited the house. Every moment he felt a Mary-shaped absence in the room. Yes, he loved her, but he had survived without her before. He could live without her again. He must.

Fitz stood abruptly, wincing at the sudden pain in his injured leg. He must cease these maudlin thoughts. He and Mary had enjoyed a brief friendship. He had been fooling himself to imagine it might be love. It was the damned enforced idleness. Once he was able to ride and shoot again, he would not succumb to such sentimentality.

Books were stacked on the table next to his bed. He had read them all, many more than once. He was weary of reading and weary of his bed. His doctor still warned him to stay abed, so Fitz had not ventured further than his sitting room on his crutches. But he refused to dress for the sick bed; now at least he wore decent trousers, a shirt, and waistcoat. It made him look less like an invalid, but nothing could make him *feel* less like an invalid.

Fitz sighed in resignation. Perhaps he would not mind reading *Robinson Crusoe* once more. He took one hobbling step toward the bed and then stopped, arrested by the sound of wheels and horses' hooves crunching on the gravel of the circular drive in front of the house. A carriage was arriving at Woodley Park. Who could it be? His mother had said nothing of anticipating visitors.

He returned to the window and took the window seat. At least it would provide a minute or two of diversion.

He was surprised to see his mother, Mary, Elizabeth, and Darcy emerge from the house, accompanied by a few liveried footmen. Why would Mary and the Darcys greet his parents' guests?

The man who emerged from the carriage was unfamiliar to Fitz. He was young, broad-shouldered, and blond, moving with an ease that Fitz, in his current hobbled state, envied. Darcy shook the man's hand enthusiastically while Mary and Elizabeth curtsied. Addressing Elizabeth, the man received a warm smile from her. Then, to Fitz's astonishment, he took Mary's hand and kissed the back tenderly—holding it for far longer than was proper, in Fitz's opinion. Mary smiled and....Good Lord, did she actually blush at this strange man's attentions?

Whoever he was, the man was clearly acquainted with all three people. A horrible thought struck Fitz. What if he was a suitor of Mary's? Or could they already be betrothed? Surely Darcy would have mentioned a betrothal even if he did not realize that Fitz had any particular interest in Mary. But she could have suitors Darcy did not know about.

He watched the figures until they disappeared into the house's entrance and then lingered to observe the footman take in the man's trunk. The carriage had a crest that he did not recognize and was well turned out. A man with a title and some means. Fitz's stomach twisted in knots.

Resolutely, he shifted his eyes away from the window. This had nothing to do with him.

What were they about downstairs? Was the man kissing Mary's hand again? What room would the newcomer occupy?

What a terrible time to be confined to his room! "Damnation!"

Fitz seized his crutches, tucked them under his arms, and hobbled to the door. He would not remain trapped here. He would not!

***

Lord Louis DeVere's arrival had been a surprise.

Mary had spent some time in the lord's company in Hertfordshire, but she had believed he called at Longbourn for Kitty's sake. With his blond hair, bright blue eyes, and broad shoulders, he was quite handsome. She and Lord DeVere had often been left behind to somewhat private conversations when Kitty and her friends were following after assorted men in regimentals, and she had assumed the lord had endured her company out of politeness.

He had chanced to visit Longbourn the day before her departure for Pemberley, and she had mentioned a possible visit to Woodley Park. It appeared that Lord DeVere's family was friendly with the Earl of Matlock's, and somehow he had obtained an invitation to visit their home. Had Lord DeVere followed her? The idea seemed preposterous, but it was difficult to dismiss entirely.

No, it was foolishness to believe that a handsome man would travel so great a distance just to be in her presence; he could easily have awaited her return to Longbourn.

Upon disembarking from his carriage, however, he had stared at her quite boldly, his eyebrows lowered. And she believed his lips had lingered over-long on her hand. Or was it all her wishful imagination?

Mary followed Lady Matlock as she showed Lord DeVere to the blue drawing room where he could take refreshments after his long journey. They conversed amiably about his father's health and common acquaintances. The two families must have been on intimate terms for quite some time. Of course, he was visiting old family friends, and Mary's presence was merely a pleasant coincidence.

However, as Lord DeVere seated himself, he happened to glance about, and his eyes fastened on Mary, sweeping appreciatively from the crown of her head to her slippers. Mary's eyebrows lifted in surprise, and she cast her eyes to the floor lest others notice her shock. She hastened to take the chair furthest from him, but when she felt equal to looking up once more, the lord's eyes were still upon her.

"So, Miss Bennet, how have you enjoyed Derbyshire so far?" he inquired.

Certain she was blushing a bright red, Mary swallowed. "It is lovely. In truth, I have seen but little of it."

"What? You have not seen the Peaks!" he cried. Mary shook her head. "That is indeed a crime!"

Lord DeVere's exclamations had attracted Elizabeth and William's attention; Mary wished she could disappear into the upholstery of her chair. "I do not mind. Mr. Darcy's cousin is recovering from an injury, and we are here to visit him."

"How dull for you!" Lord DeVere's voice held not only solicitude for her well-being but also a note of self-assurance. "I will rectify this situation. We simply *must* have an excursion to the Peaks."

Mary wished to explain that her visit had been anything but dull, and she had no present desire to be anywhere other than Woodley Park. But how would another person understand? Apart from Elizabeth, nobody knew she had visited the colonel's room, and that must remain a secret. If she did express excessive concern about the colonel's recovery, it might give rise to erroneous assumptions about the nature of their acquaintance. "I am sure that would be lovely," she murmured.

Lord DeVere inclined his head. "The Peaks are indeed—"

His words were cut off as the door flew open suddenly. With disheveled hair and a flushed face, Colonel Fitzwilliam stood in the doorway, propped up by a pair of crutches. Mary stifled a gasp. He must have exerted tremendous effort to reach the drawing room; even now he swayed a bit and seized the door jamb for support.

The colonel said nothing but first gazed intently at Mary and then glanced at Lord DeVere. Had he come all this way simply to greet a new guest?

"Richard!" Lady Matlock exclaimed. "Why have you abandoned your room?"

The colonel hobbled across the floor to the chair next to Mary's but did not yet sit. "I wished to greet our guest."

"But—"

"I grow weary of my room," he continued.

"Quite understandable!" Lord DeVere exclaimed. "I would tire of it as well."

"Richard, you remember Lord Louis DeVere? Viscount DeVere's eldest?" Lady Matlock gestured to the new guest.

"Ah, yes!" The colonel's smile seemed a bit forced. "You have changed a bit since I last saw you; I believe you were then nine years of age." Awkwardly, he maneuvered himself into the chair and laid his crutches on the floor. Mary wondered if he experienced much pain. Why had he ventured out of his room when he should be resting his leg?

Lord DeVere nodded and smiled. "Yes, we were frequent visitors here until my father's illness forced us to stay at home for many years. But at last he was granted a full recovery."

"I am glad to hear it."

"The family has been to visit several times in recent years, but you were away," Lady Matlock said.

"I am sorry to have missed you." The colonel was a most amiable man, but somehow the smile he bestowed on Lord DeVere did not quite reach his eyes. He could not possibly dislike a man whom he had not seen for so many years. What could be the cause of this reserve?

Lord DeVere settled himself into his chair, looking away from the colonel. "Yes, um, I just discovered that Miss Bennet has been confined to Woodley Park all this time and not seen the Peaks."

The colonel regarded her unhappily. "That is a shame," he murmured. Did he feel guilty that she had stayed at Woodley Park? How did she indicate to him that she did not mind?

Before she could say anything, Lord DeVere spoke again. "We must have an expedition to the Peaks, do you not agree, Colonel?"

Mary could see the muscles in the colonel's jaw straining. "Yes, indeed. A most worthwhile endeavor." The poor man! He could not climb the Peaks until he was fully healed. Of course, it had not occurred to Lord DeVere when he suggested the excursion.

"Should we venture out tomorrow?" the lord asked.

Mary's heart raced. She did not wish to undertake such an activity until the colonel could join them, but how could she say so? Before anyone else could speak, she said, "I have been experiencing a trifling cold." Elizabeth's head turned sharply toward her, and her eyes widened at this news. "Perhaps we could wait a few days."

"Yes, yes, of course!" Lord DeVere exclaimed.

The conversation immediately turned to inquiries about Mary's health and recommendations for home remedies. She fended off two offers to send for a doctor. Through it all, the colonel watched her with an unreadable expression on his face, saying nothing.

Chapter 7

Darcy visited Fitz's room faithfully every morning, and his cousin eagerly anticipated his visits. Fitz was quick to dispense with the pleasantries about the state of his health and eager to pursue questions that had been preying on his mind all night. "What do you know of this DeVere fellow?" he asked without preamble.

Darcy's eyes widened. "Not much. He is a neighbor of the Bennets. The DeVere family is respectable enough. He seems like a pleasant, well-mannered gentleman."

"Is he well off?" Fitz studied the cuff of his coat in a—probably vain—attempt to make his inquiries seem casual.

"Elizabeth says the family has a moderate fortune."

"And he is not prone to drinking or gambling?"

"No, he seems a sober enough fellow."

Damnation! The man was perfection itself. Fitz resisted the urge to pound his fist on the arm of the chair. Belatedly, he noticed Darcy regarding him with a raised eyebrow.

After a brief pause, Fitz straightened his coat and leaned back in the chair. "I am simply concerned for Miss Bennet's welfare."

Darcy's brow furrowed. "Mary?"

"Do you not believe he shows an interest in her?"

Darcy had an abstracted air as if he were considering the possibility for the first time. "I suppose it is possible. Elizabeth said they were a great deal in company together at Longbourn, and his visit here is somewhat precipitous."

The churning in Fitz's stomach increased in intensity. "Do you believe she returns his interest?"

Darcy frowned, stroking his chin. "That I cannot say. She appreciated his company and certainly was amiable in her conversation. But Mary is often a closed book."

"Hmph." Fitz attempted to settle his leg into a more comfortable position, but his whole body was as tense as a bowstring.

"He would be an excellent match for her," Darcy observed blandly.

"I am well aware of it," Fitz growled. "But they have not been acquainted long." Again he shifted, unable to relax.

"What is your interest in the matter?" Darcy turned a sharp stare on his cousin.

Fitz quickly averted his gaze to the window lest his eyes betray him. "Mar—Miss Bennet has been friendly to me. I would not wish to see her marry the wrong man."

During the ensuing silence, Fitz sought a new topic of conversation. He did not like how his cousin watched him. Darcy was far too clever for his own good. Or Fitz's.

"This weather—" Fitz began.

Darcy interrupted. "Are you interested in Miss Bennet for your own sake?"

Incensed at this effrontery, Fitz prepared to issue a firm denial. "Um...I...ah..." Somehow his mouth did not appear to be cooperating with the plan of disavowing all interest in Mary.

"Are you?" Darcy leaned forward in his chair.

Darcy feels responsible for Mary, Fitz realized. The Bennet sisters had no brother to watch over them. Naturally, Darcy would appoint himself to that role.

"You know my situation, Darcy," Fitz threw up his hands. *Why bother discussing this?* "I have no inheritance, and my situation has only grown more desperate. It is likely this injury will force me from my chosen occupation. I cannot declare myself when I have nothing to offer a woman."

Darcy bolted upright. "But Mary has a dowry."

Yes, he was aware that the Bennet daughters would receive a small sum but hardly enough to meet their needs. Fitz waved dismissively. The amount was not worth mentioning.

Darcy ran his fingers through his hair. "You do not understand. I dowered both Kitty and Mary after I married Elizabeth. Twenty thousand. Each."

Fitz restrained an urge to whistle at the impressive sum. He also restrained any errant feelings of hope. He had no desire to live on his cousin's charity. The thought made Fitz's skin crawl after years of dependence on his parents.

Oblivious to Fitz's reaction, Darcy continued. "Mr. Bennet did not wish to make the dowries general knowledge so the girls would not be targets of fortune hunters."

"Does Mary know?" Fitz asked.

Darcy shrugged. "Her father might have kept the knowledge from her. He does not have a high opinion of the intelligence of his younger girls."

Fitz stared out the window, wishing he could pace—it always helped him think. He had not permitted himself to dwell on his unexpected reaction to Mary Bennet, but he was forced to admit that she affected him quite differently than other women.

Her thoughtful, quiet presence soothed him—so unlike his boisterous army friends or a mother who had definite opinions about the course of her younger son's life. He had not thought to wed for a while yet, had not thought he *could* wed for a while yet. But if he were so inclined…

Then he remembered his present state of penury and why he had resolved not to think of Mary.

"What are your intentions toward Mary?" Darcy's voice interrupted his musings.

Fitz shifted in his seat. "My intentions? I have not said or done anything improper." Fortunately, Darcy remained unaware of Mary's secret visits, or he would demand they marry immediately.

Darcy laughed. "Fitz, you are hardly the sole of propriety!"

"I flirt with widows and barmaids, yes. But I would never treat a woman like Miss Bennet less than honorably!" Darcy winced, and Fitz realized that he was practically shouting.

What the hell is wrong with me? First I brood like the hero in a popular novel, and then I yell at my best friend for no good reason. His hands clamped down on his knees. He had to regain control of himself.

"I apologize. I did not mean to suggest—" Darcy began.

Fitz waved away the apology. "Never mind. I apologize for my outburst."

Darcy nodded to acknowledge this. He stared at the fireplace for a moment, rubbing his chin. "If your interest in Mary is serious, you should not allow considerations of income to interfere."

Easier to say if you have never worried about your income, Fitz thought bitterly.

"Her dowry—"

"Perhaps I do not wish to live off your largesse for the rest of my life, Darcy!" Fitz exploded.

Darcy's head jerked up and back. "There is no shame in accepting her dowry. Many men do so."

"Most dowries come from fathers!" Fitz hissed in reply. "It is quite a different matter when my own cousin is the source." Fitz could have accepted money from his father—after all, he had done so all his life—but somehow the thought of taking it from Darcy was...intolerable. He could not articulate the difference, but it was impossible to deny.

Darcy dropped his head, staring at his hands clasped in his lap. "I suppose so." But Fitz could see that his cousin did not truly understand. Darcy had always possessed his own fortune; he had never been dependent on anyone. Darcy spread his hands wide. "I wish I could do more to help you."

Fitz's mind again reviewed his financial realities, seeking an overlooked solution to the problem, but he found nothing. "I do as well," he sighed.

"Very well," Darcy said finally.

And they left it at that.

***

Lord DeVere had now been visiting Woodley Park for five days, and Mary had grown more and more confident of his interest in her. He sought her opinion in conversation and actively listened to her thoughts. As he entered a room, his eyes would seek hers. He solicited her playing on the pianoforte and praised it extravagantly. And he said outrageously flattering and untrue things about her beauty.

Yes, she had determined that he was courting her, but she was unsure how she felt about it.

Oh, she was flattered. Lord DeVere was not the most handsome man in Hertfordshire, but he was certainly quite eligible, and many local women had cast longing glances his way. Since his family had one of the grander estates near Meryton, his attentions to her were quite a compliment. He was polite, well-spoken, and kind.

There was nothing wrong with Lord DeVere. He would be, in every respect, an excellent choice for a husband.

Except that Mary's thoughts always turned to Colonel Fitzwilliam.

The colonel had joined the assembled party every day in the afternoon but had otherwise been absent. The simple effort of hobbling to the drawing room and participating in conversation made him appear gray and exhausted. Unsurprisingly, he was not available for dinner or daily walks in the garden or grounds.

When the colonel did join them, Mary would frequently catch his eyes on her before he quickly glanced away. What did it mean? He could not afford to show interest in a practically penniless woman. Why stare at her now?

But when she thought about him...

Mary was forced to admit to herself that her eyes often lingered on his form. He might not be a conventionally handsome man, but his face was lively and amiable. She knew how difficult it must be for a soldier to be so incapacitated, but he faced it with humor and optimism, never complaining.

Occasionally, he would engage her in a conversation about the progress of the war, which she followed through the daily paper. He provided insights that she could not have gleaned from mere written accounts. Their conversations were fascinating. But more than that, he expected her to be interested in the subject and to understand it. *He admires my intelligence!* Strangely, being admired for her intelligence appealed to her even more than being admired for her beauty.

But he will never propose to you, she reminded herself again and again. It was pointless to become enamored with the man; nothing would ever come of it.

So, on the sixth day of his visit, when Lord DeVere asked Mary to accompany him on a private walk of the Matlocks' formal gardens, she said yes.

Chapter 8

Fitz massaged his leg, emitting an oath when he kneaded a particularly tender spot. He had morning and afternoon regimens of walking and exercise. Having just completed his morning routine, he wanted to alleviate the soreness of muscles unused to such activity.

Damnation! The pain should be improving by now. When it did, he could join the others at dinner every night. But by then he customarily needed to take his dose of laudanum, which inevitably made him sleep—like a small child abed early each night.

He had been pondering his conversation with Darcy since the previous day. But today fresh doubts had crept in. Would Mary would have any interest in a lame, about-to-be ex-soldier? What did he have to offer her? Perhaps he should simply bow out and allow DeVere to have the field.

The following shudder had nothing to do with the pain in his leg. He could not deny a different sort of pain at the thought of losing her.

Without warning, the door to his room burst open, and Darcy rushed in, wide-eyed and disheveled. Pain be damned, Fitz surged to his feet.

Darcy stood in the doorway, regaining his breath. Fitz's sense of alarm increased by the second. When Darcy said nothing, Fitz was forced to ask. "What is wrong? Is someone hurt?"

"The window of our bedchamber overlooks the garden," Darcy managed to gasp out.

This was the urgent message Darcy rushed in to deliver? Fitz attempted to maintain a polite tone. "Does it?"

Darcy ran his hands through his unruly hair. "I happened to glance out a moment ago and saw Mary with Lord DeVere."

"Oh?" Now Fitz's teeth were grinding. But he turned away from his cousin. He wanted no details, and he could hardly object to a casual stroll by two people wholly unconnected to him.

Darcy stopped Fitz with a hand on his arm. "That is not all. DeVere got down on one knee!"

A great hole seemed to have opened in Fitz's chest, threatening his ability to breathe.

Darcy stared at him. "Good God, Fitz! You are as white as a ghost!"

Fitz ignored this. "I am too late. I waited too long." In a blinding flash, he realized what he wanted. He wanted Mary…beside him for the rest of his life. He could imagine no other possible future.

"Perhaps not," Darcy said. "We do not know her response."

"But if she said yes—"

Darcy's hand was a comforting weight on Fitz's shoulder. "I believe she may return your feelings."

"Has she spoken of—?"

Darcy shook his head. "I have seen how she regards you. It is nothing like her attention to DeVere."

"It could simply be pity." Fitz rubbed his forehead, sensing the beginning of a headache.

"I suppose." Darcy gave him a level gaze. "Or it could be tender regard."

Fitz's body remained frozen in place, unable to decide on a course of action. What could be done? What did he wish to do?

Fitz felt compelled to voice the treacherous thought in his head. "DeVere has far more to offer her than I do."

Darcy shook his head. "More money, perhaps. But I believe you could offer her more happiness."

Fitz gazed at his cousin. Could Darcy be correct?

"If you hurry, you might be able to propose instead." Darcy's voice had a new note of urgency.

"Or be the first to wish them happy," Fitz said bitterly.

Darcy sighed in exasperation. "Would you rather live with a lifetime of regret?"

Fitz contemplated this question for all of a second. Faced with the prospect of losing Mary, all his objections about the origin of her dowry melted away. "Oh, Good Lord! What if I am too late?" He looked at Darcy in panic.

"Hurry!" Darcy urged him.

That was when Fitz discovered, to his surprise, that he was capable of running.

***

Mary had not realized that proposals involved quite so much discussion.

Lord DeVere had lowered himself to one knee as soon as they had arrived at the bench nestled in the middle of Woodley Park's garden. The bench itself reminded her of that golden day when she had first met the colonel, but otherwise everything was different. The Matlocks' gardens were formal and exquisitely maintained. Sitting on the bench, Mary was drenched in sunlight. The garden consisted of sculpted bushes and rigidly organized borders of ornamental plants surrounding beds of decorously colored flowers. Even the gravel of the pathways seemed orderly and uniform in size and color. Hanging vines and overgrown bushes would not dare to take root at Woodley Park.

Lord DeVere was obviously leading up to asking a momentous question; however, beforehand, he felt it incumbent on himself to discuss his family's financial situation, his father's health, and his own prospects. Then he had described the qualities he sought in a future life companion, some of which provoked Mary's bemusement. She was uncertain what to think of a man who not only believed she possessed "a constitution strong enough to bear many children" but also articulated that sentiment as part of his proposal. Was it, in truth, a compliment when he declared her to be "pretty, but not too pretty" or that her figure was "ample, but not too ample"?

All of his words were embellished with very ornate language, which he seemed to consider appropriate for such a solemn occasion. She did not mind his excessive loquaciousness, although admittedly, she did not attend closely to every word he spoke. The extra time gave her a chance to consider her response to the question Lord DeVere was about to ask. What would she say?

The rational course would be to accept his offer. She had no other prospects and might never attract another suitor—except for the colonel, who would never propose, so he was not a true suitor.

I shall accept him, she resolved, ignoring the queasiness in her stomach.

He was handsome, wealthy, kind. He honored her with his attentions. She should be pleased. Why was she not more pleased?

"—Do me the honor of being my wife?"

Oh! Her attention had drifted, and she had missed the actual proposal. Should she consider that a bad sign?

Lord DeVere gazed up at her with a hopeful, tentative smile, and all Mary could think was that his knee must hurt after kneeling on the gravel pathway for so long.

What should I say? I had resolved to accept him, but—

Although she was not quite sure what response would emerge, Mary opened her mouth to speak. But she was immediately distracted by the sound of swift steps crunching the gravel; someone was arriving from the house. Who was coming at such a determined pace?

In the next moment, Colonel Fitzwilliam rounded the bush, blocking Mary's view of the path. He was obviously rushing, and without his crutches, his bad leg produced a very lopsided, painful-looking limp. His face was white and drawn; of course, it must have been very painful for him to walk so rapidly. But that would not explain the wild, fierce spark in his eyes. *Why was he jeopardizing his recovery in such a way?*

"Colonel!" she exclaimed.

Lord DeVere swore and struggled into a standing position, turning to face the colonel.

Her first thought was that someone was severely injured. Elizabeth? William? "Is there an urgency?" she asked.

He shook his head vigorously. "No, no. Nothing like that." The colonel seemed transfixed by the sight of the two of them.

Mary felt a sudden rush of frustration. He could have jeopardized his convalescence! "Why are you here? And without your crutches?"

"I-I…that is… I wanted—" He stuttered to a halt and simply blinked at Mary.

Next to her, Lord DeVere muttered an oath under his breath. "Out with it, man!" he spat out.

Rather than disconcert the colonel, the other man's rudeness seemed to stiffen his resolve. He stood straighter, lifting his chin. Ignoring the lord, he turned pleading eyes on Mary. "Please do not marry him."

Mary's mouth dropped open. How had he known?

The colonel took a few determined steps toward her, managing to stand tall despite the limp. "Do not accept him. Do not marry him. *Marry me.*" His eyes blazed the kind of fierce determination that Mary imagined him displaying on the battlefield.

"But-but you must marry an heiress."

He gave a short, angry shake of his head. "I was a fool to think so. I must marry the woman I love."

Mary's heart lurched sideways, but her head could not accept her sudden good fortune. "And that is me? Are you certain?"

The colonel laughed. "Yes, I am certain that it is you. I cannot imagine anyone else."

Hope swelled inside Mary's chest so great that her body might not contain it. "You love me?"

He took another step, close enough to clasp both her hands in his. "Passionately. Without reservation. I cannot offer you much but a modest life with a broken-down soldier, but I can offer you a lifetime of love."

And that, Mary realized, was far more than Lord DeVere—with his long-winded speeches—could promise.

"If there is any possibility you might return that feeling—"

"There is." Mary dared to interrupt him. "A possibility I mean." *Oh, what am I saying? I am making a hash of this!* "What I mean to say is I do love you. And yes, I will marry you."

The colonel—Richard—exhaled forcefully as if he had been holding his breath. His slight, amazed smile grew until he was grinning broadly. "I am—I am—overcome." The next moment, she was enfolded in his arms, and he was kissing her passionately.

Never having been kissed before, Mary had often wondered why people found the activity so pleasurable. It seemed like such an odd practice. And when she had touched her own lips, it never produced any particular sensations of pleasure.

However, when Richard's mouth slanted over hers, she suddenly found that she could think of nothing but the feeling of his lips and the very masculine scent of his body. *Now I understand all the fuss*, she thought.

And that was her last rational thought as Richard pressed his tongue against her lips, and she opened them without hesitation. The sensations she experienced then…she had no idea such feelings even existed, and she would have been hard-pressed to find words to describe them.

Too soon, Richard brought the kiss to a close, pulling back slightly to peer down at her with a slight frown. Was he concerned that he had taken liberties? But, oh—Mary could think of only one thing. "Why are you stopping? I do not wish to stop."

Richard chuckled, a rich, warm sound, and bent his head to hers once more. When they finally ceased kissing altogether, it was from lack of air, not lack of desire.

Only then did Mary remember— "Oh! Lord DeVere!" *Had he witnessed their indiscreet behavior?*

She whirled around, scanning the garden, but he was nowhere to be seen. "I never actually answered his proposal," Mary observed.

Richard laughed. "I believe he may have guessed your response."

Mary could not help smiling. "I suppose so. But I cannot help feeling...I did not mean to treat him so thoughtlessly. Although I must say he seemed more interested in how many children I could bear than anything particular about me."

Richard looked down at her with shining eyes. "I cannot find it in my heart to feel excessively guilty. This is the way it was meant to be."

She could not help returning his smile. "Indeed it is."

Epilogue

"Ooo, Lieutenant! Regimentals do make a man ever so dashing!"

Mary could not hide her smile as she overheard Kitty exclaiming over Lieutenant Broadmoor, one of the friends whom Richard had invited to their wedding. The unfortunate lieutenant smiled and drifted toward a door leading to the garden, but Mary could have warned him that nowhere at Longbourn was safe from Kitty. Of course, Mary had not chosen Richard for his red coat, but that did not prevent Kitty from pouting or expressing her determination to "find a soldier of her own."

Ironically, their marriage had prompted Richard to give up soldiering, and he planned to sell his commission as soon as they returned from their honeymoon.

Richard approached, handing her a cup of punch. "I must thank you for freeing me from Kitty's attentions."

Mary smiled up at him. "My pleasure." He took the opportunity to place a small kiss on her lips. "Richard!" she whispered, certain she was turning unattractive shades of red.

Her new husband surveyed the people who were circulating in the drawing room as they awaited the wedding breakfast. "I am certain they will forgive us a small lapse of propriety on our wedding day."

Mary glanced about, but no one seemed to be paying them particular attention. Richard leaned down until his lips brushed her ear, sending shivers down her spine. "However, in deference to your sensibilities, I will save future 'lapses' for tonight."

Despite what she suspected was a violent blush, Mary gathered up her tattered dignity and drew herself up to her full height. "Yes, that would be for the best." But she could not maintain her haughty demeanor without immediately collapsing into laughter, which infected Richard as well.

Elizabeth and William joined them as Mary was still chuckling and wiping tears from her eyes. "Now, none of that," Elizabeth admonished with a twinkle in her eye. "Weddings are a solemn occasion."

"Hmm…" Mary said. "I do remember a particular sister of mine laughing so hard at *her own* wedding breakfast that she spilled tea on her new husband's cravat."

Elizabeth affected her best innocent expression. "I cannot imagine whom you are speaking of!"

William regarded the women's byplay fondly, then turned his attention to Richard. "When may we expect the pleasure of your company at Pemberley?"

Richard's arm wrapped around Mary's waist. "We will be on our honeymoon for two weeks, and then we will stop at Pemberley."

Mary was very excited about the trip. They would see the Lakes, an area she had never visited before. Their trip would end in Derbyshire. In lieu of the dowry Mary had never known she possessed, William had given the newlyweds a small estate near Pemberley. Lark Haven Manor had been part of the Darcy lands but was not included in the entail.

Richard had been very pleased with the arrangement. Possessing an estate meant that he could be master of his own fate and leave a legacy for their children. The Darcys were also pleased to have Mary and Richard settled so near Pemberley—

and the feeling was mutual. Elizabeth had recently learned she was with child, and Mary was happily anticipating a new niece or nephew.

"I did not see Lord DeVere among the guests," Elizabeth observed to Mary.

Mary shook her head. "We did invite him, but he declined."

"I suppose it is not much of a surprise," Elizabeth said.

Lord DeVere had left Woodley Park rather precipitously following their engagement. Richard's mother had expressed surprise; no one save the Darcys, Mary, and Richard ever knew the truth behind his sudden departure. Mary had encountered the man twice at social events, and he had been cordial but distant. Recent rumors had him courting Maria Lucas despite his lack of a red coat.

Mary's thoughts were interrupted by a shrill cry. "Lieutenant! Lieutenant!" Kitty raced across the room toward Richard's friend with no concern for propriety or guests' toes.

Mary winced and shook her head. Would her sister never learn to behave in a suitable fashion?

Richard smiled and pulled her closer to him. "Do not be too harsh with Kitty, my dear. After all, if it were not for her love of red coats, I might never have ventured into the Longbourn garden and met you."

"That would indeed be a shame," William observed.

"Yes," Richard agreed with his cousin, but his eyes remained fixed on his new wife. "For when I met you, I fell in love."

The End

Please enjoy this excerpt from Victoria Kincaid's novel

Mr. Darcy to the Rescue

1

"…And now nothing remains for me but to assure you in the most animated language of the violence of my affection!"

It must be admitted that Elizabeth Bennet's attention had drifted a little as her cousin, Mr. Collins, had enumerated at great length his reasons for choosing to marry and why he had very rationally selected Elizabeth for this "honor."

Now as Elizabeth focused on his words, she had to stifle a laugh at the idea that his affection for her was violent or deep or anything more than nonexistent. In fact, he had not even managed to produce any "animated language." Instead, he had merely assured her that his language was animated. It was a bit like having someone declare it was raining when you stood in bright sunshine.

Oh, merciful heavens, he was still talking! "To fortune I am perfectly indifferent, and you may assure yourself that no ungenerous reproach shall ever pass my lips when we are married." As he drew breath for another long-winded speech, Elizabeth knew she must say something—and quickly!

"You are too hasty, sir! You forget that I have not yet made an answer—"

Mr. Collins waved his hand airily. "We may dispense with these formalities. We both know how you shall respond."

"We do?" Elizabeth expected smoke to be streaming from her ears by now.

"Yes, I have spoken with your most excellent father, and he assured me how felicitous he found this event." He graced her with a smile, which presumably was intended to be charming, but oozed insincerity.

"He did?" Elizabeth found these words hard to credit.

"Indeed. I assured him that our union is already a foregone conclusion since we are united of one mind and one heart."

"We are?" Elizabeth could not stay silent any longer. "Pray, sir, when did that happen?"

Mr. Collins merely looked bemused. "I...do not believe I can supply you with the exact date...."

Elizabeth shrugged. "I keep a journal. I shall have to go back to see if I recorded it." She tapped her lip with her finger. "I hope it did not escape my notice."

Her erstwhile suitor blinked rapidly, fiddling with his cuffs. "Your father did caution me that you should speak with him first before making any decision regarding my most generous offer." He shrugged. "I do not see the necessity since we both know that another offer of marriage may never be made to you... Miss Elizabeth?"

Mr. Collins had been so caught up in the sound of his own voice that it took him a few moments to realize that Elizabeth was halfway across the drawing room floor. He hastened to catch up with her. "Where are you going, my most precious love blossom?"

The sound of this ridiculous pet name almost stopped Elizabeth altogether, but she had a more urgent mission. "I must speak with my father," she muttered.

"Why?"

"To assure myself his wits are in order."

"Hmm?" Mr. Collins's tone was quizzical. "I assure you he was of quite sound mind this morning when I spoke to him."

Briefly, Elizabeth considered the possibility that Mr. Collins was so stupid he was incapable of being insulted. Elizabeth would be tempted to laugh if the situation were not so dire. Why would her father give Mr. Collins the impression he wanted her to marry him?

She opened the door to her father's study rather more forcefully than she intended, and it banged against the wall. Her father looked up from his desk as Elizabeth closed the door, preventing Mr. Collins from entering.

"Ah, Lizzy, I thought I might receive a visit from you." Elizabeth's father removed his spectacles and regarded his daughter with a grim smile.

Elizabeth sat in the chair opposite the desk but perched on the edge, unable to relax. She expected Papa to smile and laugh or at least regard her with an ironic twinkle in his eye. Instead, he merely looked worn and solemn. "Mr. Collins has made me an offer of marriage." Her voice trembled with uncertainty.

"And you listened to him?"

"I suppose I must be amenable to people's wishes some of the time, or I run the danger of becoming predictable."

Such banter usually drew a chuckle from her father, but today, it merely produced a rather wan smile. Fingers of anxiety crept up Elizabeth's spine. "Papa, is there something amiss?"

Her father's hands fiddled with his spectacles. "The last thing I wanted was to burden you with this. If Mr. Bingley had… Well, it is of no matter."

Elizabeth said nothing. Everyone in the family had been disappointed when Mr. Bingley had abruptly left the neighborhood two days earlier. Jane tried to hide her melancholy, but the loss still haunted her eyes. Elizabeth still believed that Mr. Bingley would return, but his sister's latest letter to Jane had held little hope.

Papa rubbed his hand over his forehead wearily. "Do you recall when Mr. Bartlett was here a week ago?" Elizabeth nodded. She had sent for the doctor herself after her father experienced pains in his chest. "I may have misled your mother about how severe he believes the problem to be."

Elizabeth's breath caught.

"Mr. Bartlett believes my heart is weakening. And it is only a matter of time until it fails." Papa's voice was calm, but his hands moved restlessly over the surface of the desk.

Elizabeth covered her mouth to muffle her gasp. "Oh, Papa!" Tears spilled out of her eyes and ran unchecked down her cheeks.

Her father nodded slowly. "I know. I am not a young man. I had hoped for more time, but..." His hands once again worried the frame of his spectacles. "For my own sake, I have made peace with it, but I do wish you girls could be safely married." He ran his hand through the thinning hair over his forehead; many strands of gray had recently joined the strands of brown. "I had intended to father a son. And when it became clear that was not to be..." He bowed his head, showing the weight of his years. "I should have run my business affairs more carefully. That is the truth."

"Oh no, Papa!" Lizzy cried. She jumped up and hurried around the desk so she could kneel beside her father's chair. "'Tis nothing but the vagaries of fate! Our situation can scarcely be laid at your door."

"If it pleases you to say it…." Her father patted the hand she laid on his arm. "I must confess to being a coward as well. I have not shared this news with your mother. I did not wish her to worry—or shriek." Elizabeth and her father exchanged a knowing look.

Elizabeth stood, leaning against the desk for support. "Do not be anxious for our future. The solution has been presented to us just in time." She swallowed hard. "I shall marry Mr. Collins and then when you…" She noticed a tremor in her voice. "And then Mama and my sisters will not be forced to leave Longbourn. It is the perfect solution."

Her father leaned back into his chair, looking very frail. "Yes, indeed, it would be perfect if Mr. Collins were a sensible person. If he were not living proof that the Good Lord has a sense of humor. But I would not ask you to make such a sacrifice! I would have you marry for love." The corners of his lips, indeed his whole face, seemed to be dragged down by the weight of his burdens.

"You are not asking; I am offering. Yes, I had hoped for love, but I have always known the chances of finding it were never very great. I am much too outspoken, and I have little dowry. I love Longbourn and my family, so I would be marrying for a different kind of love." She attempted to catch her father's eye, but his head remained bowed.

"Perhaps Mr. Collins's affections might be transferred to one of the other girls…"

Elizabeth took her father's cold hand in hers, touched by how much he cared for her. "Mary has stated more than once in Mr. Collins's presence that she has no intention of ever marrying. Kitty and Lydia are too young and silly. And Jane… I could not ask that of her." Elizabeth wanted to believe Mr. Bingley would return for Jane, and nothing should stand in the way of her sister's happiness.

"But—"

Elizabeth formed her lips into a semblance of a smile. "My marriage will bring happiness to you and Mama and the family. And it will ensure our future. That will make me very happy indeed." Kneeling again, she tried to radiate an air of calm acceptance, although it was not one of her strengths. *Perhaps Jane can give me lessons.*

Her father placed his other hand on hers. "I must confess it would set my mind at ease to know the family future would be secured."

"It will be." Elizabeth squeezed his fingers briefly.

Papa shifted in his seat, looking at the window. "I have said nothing of my health to anyone. I think it best if it remains that way."

"Yes, of course," Elizabeth said. Even with the promise of security through her marriage to Mr. Collins, her mother would be beside herself with anxiety. "Your health might continue to be good for quite a time. No need to worry about it now."

"Yes, just as Mr. Bartlett said." He turned his gaze back to Elizabeth. Tears glistened in the corners of his eyes. "Oh, my darling girl, you have ever been a comfort to me."

She gave her father a watery smile. "And you have been my strength, Papa."

Her father discreetly wiped his eyes and straightened in his chair. Elizabeth stood.

"Now, go and give Mr. Collins the good news. It is far more than he deserves." Her father picked up his book. "I am nearly to the end of this book, and I mean to finish it today." He managed to smile at her before lowering his eyes to the book, but he blinked rapidly as he commenced reading.

Before opening the door, Elizabeth wiped her eyes with a handkerchief, wishing to avoid awkward questions about red-rimmed eyes and blotchy skin. *Although Mr. Collins would certainly interpret them as tears of joy.*

But no, she must not be bitter. She must only dwell on the good things about the marriage. This union will make her father happy, her family happy, Mr. Collins happy. Only one person would not be happy.

But that does not matter, she told herself firmly and opened the door.

2

"I had a letter from Jane Bennet yesterday."

These words, falling from the lips of Caroline Bingley, had the power to make Darcy's gaze lurch in her direction. Was that her intent? The smirk forming on her lips suggested it might be. He turned his gaze back to the fireplace.

Darcy had invited Bingley to tea at Darcy House, and the addition of Miss Bingley to the party had been an unwelcome surprise. When she had followed her brother into the drawing room,

Bingley had given Darcy a small, apologetic shrug. Darcy was most concerned about her effect on Georgiana, who found Miss Bingley intimidating. When would Bingley ever learn to gainsay his sister?

So far, however, the afternoon had proceeded smoothly. Georgiana had not uttered a word, but at least had remained in the room. Then Miss Bingley had proceeded to introduce this sensitive topic of conversation.

Charles Bingley was hardly less interested in his sister's surprise announcement than Darcy. He shifted in his chair and set down his tea cup. "Ja-Miss Bennet wrote to you? W-what news is there from Meryton?" He made no attempt to sound casual.

Enjoying the effect she had on her listeners, his sister leaned back in her chair and drawled, "They have had a good deal of rain over the past fortnight."

Bingley rolled his eyes. "Yes. And?"

"Jane's Aunt Phillips had a cold but seems to be improving." Miss Bingley's smirk only widened.

Bingley made a frustrated noise. "Is that all?"

Darcy could sympathize. Her triumphant tone suggested she had news of great import, but perhaps she was simply teasing them. Darcy settled back in his chair and took a sip of tea.

Caroline Bingley had been the only member of their party at Netherfield who had guessed about Darcy's attraction to Elizabeth. Three months before, he had left Hertfordshire determined to forget everything about Elizabeth Bennet but had found the task far more difficult than he anticipated. Elizabeth haunted his days and nights without ceasing. During the day, his thoughts turned to her:

her musical laugh, teasing voice, light and pleasing figure. At night, he struggled to sleep, and when he did, he dreamed of her.

Again and again, he had examined the problem but had always determined there was no other solution than to banish her from his thoughts. So far, he had met with little success, and now this reminder from Miss Bingley only threatened to further disturb his equanimity.

Georgiana nibbled a biscuit, attempting to appear interested in a conversation about people she had never met.

"Caroline—" Bingley's voice held a note of warning.

Miss Bingley sighed dramatically as if extremely put out by her brother's demands. "Well… There was one item of interest. One of Jane's sisters is engaged to be married to that parson who is a cousin of theirs." Miss Bingley sneered, a singularly unattractive expression.

"Mr. Collins," Darcy supplied.

"Yes, that is his name."

Darcy's chest compressed with anxiety, making it hard to breathe. "Which sister?"

"The second. Elizabeth." Miss Bingley slid him a look that could not be interpreted as anything less than triumphant.

It was now *impossible* for Darcy to breathe. What had happened to the air in the room?

Elizabeth! Engaged to that idiot? Married to that fool for the rest of her life? Going to his bed? Bearing his children?

No! It was not possible. Darcy needed to protest the impossibility of this pronouncement, refute it immediately, but nothing emerged from his mouth save a strangled gurgle. Georgiana's gaze shifted to him, wide-eyed with alarm.

Bingley, fortunately, had not lost his powers of speech. "Engaged to Mr. Collins! I thought she had more sense."

"She does," Darcy growled. "There must be some error."

Miss Bingley's laugh held no actual mirth. "Jane would hardly make such a mistake!"

"The man is a fool!" Darcy expostulated. "How could she accept him?"

Georgiana had plastered herself against the back of her chair, her eyes never leaving his face. His outburst was out of character, he knew, but at the moment, he could not find the means to control himself.

"Now that I think of it," Bingley said, "I do recall that Collins danced two dances with her at the Netherfield Ball."

"Yes, he danced very ill!" Darcy said.

"Perhaps he had been courting her back then," Bingley concluded.

Darcy closed his eyes and considered this. The idiot parson had danced with Elizabeth and made a fool of himself. He had tried to engage her in conversation, but Darcy had seen no signs of interest on her part. Elizabeth had far too much sense. She had been mortified when Collins had presumed to converse with Darcy without an introduction. No, it was impossible. How could she have accepted his hand?

When he opened his eyes, he noticed the gaze of everyone in the room upon him. Damnation! He too easily betrayed himself when it came to Elizabeth Bennet!

Taking a bite of a biscuit he had no interest in, Darcy attempted to appear more casual. "Did Miss Bennet's letter say when the wedding is to take place?" he asked, taking a sip of tea and attempting to calm the trembling in his hands.

"No." Miss Bingley's tone was sharp.

Good Lord! They could already be wed! This thought constricted his throat, and he almost choked as he swallowed his biscuit.

"Miss Bennet did tell me that Longbourn is entailed away from the female line," Bingley said. "Mr. Collins will inherit it upon Mr. Bennet's death."

Blast! Why had he not known that Longbourn was entailed? It was a common enough practice. He should have thought to inquire. "I did not know," Darcy murmured, now feeling faintly nauseous.

Mr. Collins must have resolved to choose a wife from among his cousins since he was to inherit their home. And he did not select Jane because everyone believed she would marry Bingley….

Elizabeth would have accepted his offer for the good of her family. He had not misjudged her powers of discernment after all. She recognized the man's stupidity but sacrificed her future happiness—*all* her future happiness—so her family would not have to leave their ancestral home.

For a moment Darcy feared he might be sick. She would be married forever to man she could not love—or even respect. *What a horrible fate.*

"So she accepted the proposal for the sake of her family?" Georgiana entered the conversation for the first time. Clearly Elizabeth's dilemma had drawn his sister's compassion. *At least Georgiana would never need to make such an awful choice,*

Darcy thought warmly. *Far better she died an old maid than marry such a man.*

Bingley nodded. "Yes, I believe so."

"What a sacrifice to make!" Georgiana exclaimed. "She must be an exceptional woman."

Miss Bingley's expression turned from triumphant to sour.

"She is indeed," Darcy agreed while simultaneously wishing she were more selfish and less devoted to her family.

And now she is lost to me. Before I ever had her. My Elizabeth is gone.

Mr. Darcy to the Rescue
A Pride and Prejudice Variation

Victoria Kincaid

When the irritating Mr. Collins proposes marriage, Elizabeth Bennet is prepared to refuse him, but then she learns that her father is ill. If Mr. Bennet dies, Collins will inherit Longbourn and her family will have nowhere to go. Elizabeth accepts the proposal, telling herself she can be content as long as her family is secure. If only she weren't dreading the approaching wedding day…

Ever since leaving Hertfordshire, Mr. Darcy has been trying to forget his inconvenient attraction to Elizabeth. News of her betrothal forces him to realize how devastating it would be to lose her. He arrives at Longbourn intending to prevent the marriage, but discovers Elizabeth's real opinion about his character. Then Darcy recognizes his true dilemma…

How can he rescue her when she doesn't want him to?

What reviewers are saying…

"This novel grabbed my attention from the first page of the book and held it to the end. I was definitely hooked by the second chapter and did not want to put it down. It is a fast read but the story line is not rushed. It is well developed and complete.

Ms. Kincaid, your Mr. Darcy was true to canon with his difficulty in expressing himself but your revealing of his inner voice with such wit was delightful! I found myself charmed and laughing at his clever reflections. Well done, Victoria Kincaid. " -- *More Agreeably Engaged* A Favorite Austenesque Variation for 2015

"Another enthralling and entertaining variation by Victoria Kincaid! I greatly enjoyed the thought-provoking premise, emotional exploration, and the chance to observe Mr. Darcy rivaled against Mr. Collins! *Mr. Darcy to the Rescue* is a wonderful choice if you are looking for a creative, romantic, low-angst, and fast-paced read!" *Austenesque Reviews*

"The journey is lighthearted, fresh and funny. This is the 3rd book I've read from Victoria Kincaid, and once again she wrote a book that is never boring and that keeps urging us to read it without stopping." -- *From Pemberley to Milton*

Pride and Proposals
A Pride and Prejudice Variation

Victoria Kincaid

What if Mr. Darcy's proposal was too late?

Darcy has been bewitched by Elizabeth Bennet since he met her in Hertfordshire. He can no longer fight this overwhelming attraction and must admit he is hopelessly in love.

During Elizabeth's visit to Kent she has been forced to endure the company of the difficult and disapproving Mr. Darcy, but she has enjoyed making the acquaintance of his affable cousin, Colonel Fitzwilliam.

Finally resolved, Darcy arrives at Hunsford Parsonage prepared to propose—only to discover that Elizabeth has just accepted a proposal from the Colonel, Darcy's dearest friend in the world.

As he watches the couple prepare for a lifetime together, Darcy vows never to speak of what is in his heart. Elizabeth has reason to dislike Darcy, but finds that he haunts her thoughts and stirs her emotions in strange ways.

Can Darcy and Elizabeth find their happily ever after?

What reviewers are saying....

"Pride and Proposals is a captivating and consuming read! I loved the intense premise, skillful character development, and emotive prose Victoria Kincaid employed. I would absolutely love to read more from her in the future! I highly recommend this novel to readers looking for a sensational and impassioned variation of Pride and Prejudice!" -- *Austenesque Reviews* Austenesque Reviews Favorite Winner for 2015.

"I really enjoyed this poignant story of love and loss, loyalty, friendship and passion. The relationships among Darcy, Elizabeth and Richard are heartwarming, and the angst was offset by an underlying dry sense of humor that kept it from being too overwhelming." *–Austenprose*

"I am happy to say, this one does take on original plot twists, and offer creative solutions to this delicate situation. It was clever where it needed to be and sentimental in the right places, without feeling forced or artificial in its delivery. I want to thank Victoria Kincaid for writing such a delightful triangle story, which started my own love of this fun, and sometimes painful, sub-genre." *– JustJane1813*

The Secrets of Darcy and Elizabeth
A Pride and Prejudice Variation

Victoria Kincaid

In this *Pride and Prejudice* variation, a despondent Darcy travels to Paris in the hopes of forgetting the disastrous proposal at Hunsford. Paris is teeming with English visitors during a brief moment of peace in the Napoleonic Wars, but Darcy's spirits don't lift until he attends a ball and unexpectedly encounters…Elizabeth Bennet! Darcy seizes the opportunity to correct misunderstandings and initiate a courtship.

Their moment of peace is interrupted by the news that England has again declared war on France, and hundreds of English travelers must flee Paris immediately. Circumstances force Darcy and Elizabeth to escape on their own, despite the risk to her reputation. Even as they face dangers from street gangs and French soldiers, romantic feelings blossom during their flight to the coast. But then Elizabeth falls ill, and the French are arresting all the English men they can find….

When Elizabeth and Darcy finally return to England, their relationship has changed, and they face new crises. However, they have secrets they must conceal—even from their own families.

What reviewers are saying…

"A romantic rewrite of Jane Austen's 'Pride and Prejudice', Victoria Kincaid's version has retained the romance and essence of Ms. Austen's original work, adding more action and adventure. There is a modern depth to this romance while it remains clean and true to the time period. The addition of the Napoleonic wars and their effects fit well with the story and add to the excitement without distracting from the romance or causing unnecessary plot threads. Additionally, the writing is smooth, develops at a steady pace ….'The Secrets of Darcy and Elizabeth' is a must read for any Austen fan!" -- *InD'Tale Magazine* (Nominated for a RONE Award)

"The Secrets of Darcy and Elizabeth is an exciting, humorous, and sweet tale. Dropping Mr. Darcy and Elizabeth in Paris in such a tumultuous time in history is a unique touch, as I had no idea how that aspect of the story would play out…. I spent a couple of delightful afternoons with this novel, and I can't wait to see what Kincaid writes next." – *Diary of an Eccentric*

"The story is full of drama and can be quite serious, it is not without its humour thanks to characters such as Caroline and this Mr Fenton. I laughed many times while I was reading this! If you like a fast moving story, full to the brim of drama and adventure, with some brilliant humour and beautiful romance thrown in then this is the story for you!" -- *Laughing with Lizzie*

About Victoria Kincaid

As a professional freelance writer, Victoria writes about IT, data storage, home improvement, green living, alternative energy, and healthcare. Some of her more…unusual writing subjects have included space toilets, taxi services, laser gynecology, bidets, orthopedic shoes, generating energy from onions, Ferrari rental car services, and vampire face lifts (she swears she is not making any of this up).

Victoria has a Ph.D. in English literature and has taught composition to unwilling college students. Today she teaches business writing to willing office professionals and tries to give voice to the demanding cast of characters in her head. She lives in Virginia with her husband, two children who love to read, and an overly affectionate cat. A lifelong Jane Austen fan, Victoria confesses to an extreme partiality for the Colin Firth miniseries version of *Pride and Prejudice.*

Thank you for purchasing this book.

Your support makes it possible for authors like me to continue writing.

Please consider leaving a review where you purchased the book

or at Goodreads.com.

Learn more about me and my upcoming releases:

Website: www.victoriakincaid.com

Twitter: VictoriaKincaid@kincaidvic

Blog: https://kincaidvictoria.wordpress.com/

Facebook: https://www.facebook.com/kincaidvictoria